DARK RIVER STONE COLLECTIVE #2

WHEN
darkness
TURNS
TO *light*

JP SAYLE

Dark Angels is the family Toad chose when he follows his heart. Will one man's love and his brothers be enough to protect him from danger?

Toad has been running for years from those who locked him up and threw away the key because he is gay. An accident places the man he loves right in his path, but it also puts his life in jeopardy. Now he must face his past to claim his future.

The past forces Sid to keep his personal life separate from those he calls family, Dark Angels. That is until he invites Toad to live with him. As the other man sees beneath the barriers to what is hidden underneath, can Sid resist what Toad offers him: Unconditional Love?

When Darkness Turns to Light is an MC, MM sexy romance, where close proximity reveals that nothing is as it seems on the surface. This is the second book in the Dark River Stone Collective and can be read as a standalone.

For every reader who picks up one of my books and finds themselves transported into my head, your welcome 😊

Prologue

SID

Fury gripped me by the throat, got me out of my apartment, and onto my motorcycle. I didn't know where I was heading until I pulled up outside the bar on the outskirts of Austin, Texas.

Walking into the bar, I glanced about, and the same uneasy feeling that always came from visiting a gay bar ran through me. The place was decent, with a mix of men from different backgrounds, and no one tended to hassle anyone. The décor was geared toward cowboys more than bikers, but I wasn't fussy when I wanted to pick up a dude for the night. I wasn't a frequent visitor because I didn't often scratch the itch that said I was gay. It was a part of myself that I'd learned to control most of the time, but after the weekend, I needed an outlet for my feelings, and, unfortunately, this was it.

Hands shoved deep into the front pockets of my jeans, I kept my gaze on the bar and off the men that hung around the tables, some giving me subtle signs of interest. I walked over the hardwood floor, knowing most of them would run a fucking mile if they knew what I had in mind for my night's entertainment. It wasn't soft foreplay or trying to play nice. I needed to fuck, pure and simple. To get rid of the aggression that wouldn't take a fucking hint and go away.

When I reached the bar, the bartender I'd fucked before sauntered over, invitation blatant. "What you drinkin', honey?'" His sexy smirk offered me something I hated myself for wanting. What was his name? Den? Dean?

Fuck if I could remember. "Whatever you have on tap," I answered as I leaned against the bar, not making eye contact with any of the men sitting on the stools close by.

A minute later, a beer was pushed toward me, and I dug my hand into my back pocket to pull out my wallet.

"It's on me, honey. It's been a while since I've seen you." He offered me another of his sexy smiles that tonight did nothing more than piss me off, right along with the stupid endearment. Why did people use those ridiculous names? Had I fucked this guy once, or was it twice? I couldn't remember, and that was pitiful. Stylish blond hair and a little scruff on his chin, a slim build that I'd usually be interested in, did absolutely nothing for me. Tonight, I wanted to fuck, and hard. I'd break this guy with what I needed.

Pushing the money toward him, I ignored what he'd said and the look of disappointment on his face as he took the cash and gave me a nod. He moved away as I sipped at the beer and listened to the music that wasn't to my taste. Country music was blah and left me with nothing else to think about other than why I was sitting in a gay bar. I'd let Linc down pure and simple. I was his second in command of Dark Angels, and I should have known what the rat bastards were up to. But no, I had my head up my fucking ass trying to pretend I wasn't attracted to one of the club members. How fucked up was that?

Linc was the only one that knew I was gay, although we never talked about it. I didn't talk about that shit with anyone. Was that why I'd dropped the ball? I wanted to kick my own ass or invite Linc to, but the man was too busy having his own personal issues with his lawyer, Mason. But Linc wasn't a coward, unlike me. No, I fucking hid and came skulking to bars when the need wouldn't give my head any peace.

Being the second in a club like the Dark Angels was a big deal. It came with a lot of responsibility, but I'd gotten so tangled up in evading myself that I'd dropped the ball. The slime that had been the club's senior members had been secretly setting up the president, Linc, and it had slipped right past me. *Fucking rat-shit bastards.*

The rage that I'd contained as I'd fought next to Linc the day before just wouldn't let go. I'd wanted to kill the motherfuckers, but that wasn't what Linc had wanted, though we'd kicked ass. Right now, that was little consolation when I wanted to rip someone apart with my bare hands. Those hands shook as I lifted the pint and drank half of it straight down.

Movement at my side was the only indication someone had sat on the stool next to mine. I swallowed a groan when my nose filled with a familiar scent I'd recognize blindfolded. Why tonight? Why now?

One glance at the hands laying on the bar, tapping at the shiny counter, and my heart started to thud painfully against my ribs. The beer I'd drunk burned like battery acid as I stared into familiar eyes. Eyes I'd dreamed of more than I'd admit aloud. "What the fuck you doin' here?" I growled, low and mean.

He licked his lips, gaze not meeting mine as a dark flush appeared over his exposed skin. The deep tan didn't hide it, and neither did the scruff on his lower jaw. An unwanted flare of desire that I'd been doing my best not to acknowledge made its presence felt as the jeans I wore became snug.

Had I been right all along? Was the guy gay? *He's fucking sitting in a gay bar, dimwit.*

"Getting a drink, same as you," he answered in that low voice that never failed to set my body alight. He raised his hand to the barman to attract his attention as if to make his point. We both knew different, but right then, my mind could only think about the possibilities of what could happen if I acted on what I was feeling.

The barman served him, and I showed no interest in anyone but the man sitting next to me. This place had a reputation for discretion, and it was why I chose it when the need to fuck became too much to resist. It had been six months since I'd last been there. Why tonight? Had he followed me?

That thought fucked with my head when I wanted something different, something dark.

The silence stretched between us, as did the sexual tension. I could scent it.

Sea-blue eyes turned in my direction. "That was a bit of a clusterfuck."

He didn't need to clarify that he was talking about what had gone down yesterday. "It was."

His gaze remained on me, which was unusual as the guy tended to avoid looking directly at me most of the time, not that I paid much attention.

Yeah, you don't at all look at that fucking hotness. Imagining pinning him to a wall and fucking his brains out? The visual, and the snarky voice that often sounded like Linc, didn't let me escape what I'd wanted for months. I sighed hard. "You wanna fuck?"

The only reaction was a slight curve of one eyebrow. "That would be a mistake."

"Maybe, but right now, I'm willing to take the risk." Or my cock was.

He picked up his beer, and his full lips pressed against the glass, giving me an image of them pressing against mine. *Back the fuck up! No kissing. Fucking is what you want.*

Unease crept through me, and I acknowledged he was right. I needed to look for someone else. I shifted and glanced about the large room that was busy for a Monday night. A few men showed interest if the smiles I was getting were any indication. Still, none of them ignited the same spark as the man sitting silently next to me, watching me.

"What are you looking for?"

His gaze held me captive as the mask he wore daily slipped, and for the first time since we'd met, his face revealed what he was feeling: desire. It was powerful, and if that wasn't the yank my chain needed... "Hard and fast." I held my breath to see if I had read him right.

He gave a slow nod. "Where?"

I glanced about the bar and, for the first time in my life, I didn't want to fuck in a bathroom stall or out back in some dark alley. It was risky, but it seemed tonight, I'd lost my sanity. "My place."

I got up off the barstool, saying nothing more, and left. I didn't need to explain where that was, not when he worked in the auto shop beneath my apartment. The sound of feet thudding behind me ramped up the excitement I refused to think too hard about. Heading down the steps, I zipped up my leather jacket, even though the warmth of the air was oppressive. Once at my motorcycle, I glanced over my shoulder before I slung my leg over my hog, my cock hard and wanting.

Long and lean, the guy screamed sex, his hair fell about his gorgeous face as he slipped on his jacket. Not once did he look in my direction as he mounted his motorcycle and lifted his helmet. I followed and started the engine, enjoying the power underneath me as it throbbed and increased the need.

The night's darkness was broken only by the brightness of the stars. The scent of dry earth and heat all I could smell as Toady took off and I chased him. The wind buffed my hot face as I rode down the winding roads letting my mind clear.

Was I really doing this?

Even as the question floated through my head, I knew the answer. I'd wanted this from the second I'd laid eyes on the other man, and I hated myself for it. A homophobic ass of a father had made sure that I'd learned to hate myself from a young age. I'd always known I was gay. I couldn't say how, just that I had. When my old man was alive, I was sure he knew it too with the way he'd gone on and on, using me as his personal punching bag until I grew too big and could hit back. It was why I'd become a prospect in Dark Angels. I wanted to prove I was a man. A sinister laugh left my lips. My father would turn in his grave if he knew the president of Dark Angels was gay and dating a lawyer of all things.

That was something I hadn't been expecting. This weekend had shown just how committed both men were. When Linc had zoned out after the fight, the only man I'd thought to ring was Mason, his lawyer dealing with the shit storm that Nola had created by accusing Linc of rape. It had been the right choice, even if I'd caused more tension with club members. But fuck, I'd had to do something.

The anger was back. An ugly beast that ate at me, leaving me struggling to keep control of the motorcycle as I took the next bend a little too fast and shot past the man in front of me. The speed demon inside kept me from thinking about anything else as I rode as if the devil were chasing me.

It wasn't long before I pulled up outside the front of Stone's auto shop; the place that I part-owned with Linc. I cut the engine, and in the quiet of the night, the sound of the other bike left me glancing about the primarily industrial area before I relaxed enough to take a breath. The place was eerily quiet, not that I'd expected anything else. I was the only one who chose to live in the large unit that housed the auto shop.

A second later, a headlight lit up the building and me before it passed and disappeared around the back of the building. I wasn't sure if it were anger or excitement that caused my hands to shake. I got off the bike and followed him around the back of the building. He stood with his helmet hanging off his handlebar, his expression protected by the darkness of the night.

Silently I took the last few steps that separated us and took hold of him. I wasn't gentle as I tugged him toward me, and before I could let common sense stop me, I claimed the lips I'd dreamed about. They were softer than I'd imagined as they parted, and he groaned low and deep as I thrust my tongue deep in his mouth. The taste of the beer was there, but underlying was something else, something sweeter. My hold tightened as the taste became instantly addictive, and the desire I'd been keeping in check for months rose to obliterate any control I had left.

My chest heaved as I staggered toward the building. His body thudded hard against the brick, but he didn't complain as I continued to devour his sweet lips. I ground my pelvis against his, and we both moaned as hardness met hardness. His muscles rippled under my hands as I dragged at his leather jacket, desperate to touch him.

The need for more was the only reason I released his lips. "Inside, now," I rasped breathlessly.

He didn't argue as I unlocked the door and turned on the light. It was then that I got a good look at him. His mouth was swollen, his eyes heavy-lidded and begging for more. He was gorgeous, and I let myself, for the briefest of moments, consider that I could have more than this one night.

He moved silently past me and walked up the stairs. His firm ass flexed as his low-slung jeans cupped the hard flesh. My mouth watered for a taste. I kicked the door shut behind us and followed him.

In the apartment, I didn't bother to look around at the mess. I was single, and the girl I had clean for me wasn't scheduled till the next day. The guy didn't look anywhere but at me as he started to strip. Off came his jacket and T-shirt, followed quickly by his jeans and boots.

Fuck, he'd gone commando. My cock jerked and leaked, adding to the growing wet patch in my underwear, but I was mesmerized by the naked man in front of me. I'd imagined what he'd look like naked. This was so much fucking more. He wasn't overly big, just long, lean, and fucking gorgeous. The V that led down to his slim hips was as perfect as the eight-pack he sported, each muscle the perfect space to let cum pool in.

The cock standing proud from a trimmed patch of dark hair was long and thick. Beads of precum gathered at the tip the longer I stared at him. "You gonna stare or we gonna fuck?"

The rasped question was more of a demand, and it stoked my desire higher as I removed my clothes, keeping eye contact. The connection between us was nothing like I'd experienced before. I wasn't sure if that was because it was usually quick with limited contact.

He remained standing in the middle of my apartment, not moving as I stalked toward him, his gaze shifting to my arousal. His lips parted slightly, and he got a glazed look in his eyes that didn't hurt my ego.

"Hard and fast."

His response was a nod, and then it was game on. I dove for his mouth, unable to resist the temptation another moment. Not one for kissing; I could easily see myself wanting to do this again and again. *No. Fuck. Fucking. That's all.*

It grated as the voice of reason worked to kill what was happening inside me. I shut it out and, for the first time in my life, let go of all the barriers. I wasn't sure if he sensed the change as he went pliant in my arms. I wrapped my arms around him and lifted him, getting a moan as a reward. "Hold on."

Lean legs wrapped around my waist as I continued to kiss his lush mouth, walking through my apartment and praying I wouldn't trip the fuck over on my way to the bedroom. Or lose something much more precious: my heart.

Chapter 1

SID

As I stepped inside the auto shop, the sounds and smells of the workshop settled some of the anxious feelings I'd developed at the clubhouse. The auto shop was the place I'd used for years to get out of my head. Working on engines, whatever they were, was a passion I'd turned into a profitable business for Dark Angels and myself. The profits were split between the club, Linc, and me and, over the years, I'd invested my cash so I'd never have to worry about where the next dollar was coming from.

Angels was minus half the members, not that it turned out to be any great loss. No one wanted traitorous bastards as brothers. The code of having each other's back was not only broken; it had been fucking torn apart. I rubbed at my forehead to ease the throbbing that had started the second Linc had mentioned the changes that needed to happen at the club.

We'd avoided doing anything for the last two months while we'd waited to see what was going to happen after the dust had settled. The injuries several ex-members had sustained during a confrontation on the ride out left some in the hospital still. Not that I cared one fucking iota about the rat-shit bastards. The issue was having a mixed club, it had been that way since Linc's granddaddy had started the club. After Nola was introduced as a prospect, it had soured and tainted the club. There weren't many female members. Which was why Linc had wanted to meet in private to discuss what to do next.

"What's got you lookin' so pissed?"

A shiver of desire ran down my spine and lodged itself in a place it had no fucking business going at the silky voice. I didn't stop walking. "Everything," I spat out and refused to look at the other guy.

The scent of paint and grease followed me as I opened the door to my office then slammed it shut hard enough that the pictures on the wall rattled before settling. I rested a hand on the door as I stared at it hard enough to blister the paintwork. Why did he have to be so fucking tempting?

I shook off the simmering desire to open the door and go back out into the shop. It would do me no fucking good. I'd sworn to keep away after the one lapse in judgment, and I never went back on my word, ever. That got me to the desk and the pile of paperwork that came from running a business. It was the one part of Stone's auto shop I hated, but it was a necessary evil if we wanted to keep everything legit the way Linc wanted.

Reaching for the stack of invoices that needed inputting into the account's spreadsheet for Nutty, who did all the bookkeeping for the accountant, I swallowed the grumpy sigh and dropped the pile next to the computer. An hour later, I lifted my head at the sound of a knock on the door. "What?" I hollered.

Ram poked his head around the door. "Sid, we got an issue out here." His face was ashen, and I was up and out of the seat. Ram wasn't prone to dramatics, so the pale, sweaty face left my guts clenched.

I followed him and stopped at the sight of Toad on the far side of the shop, lying on the floor next to the bike he'd been doing a hand-painted design on. Toad had a sectioned-off area with plastic walls to prevent any shit from getting on his work. I could see his stark features as eyes as huge as plates stared up at the men starting to crowd him. I was unaware that I was running until I burst through the plastic. "Fuck, what happened?" I growled through the panic, trying to crawl through my skin as I pushed the men out of my way.

One of Toad's hands was nearly double the size and covered in angry red blisters. His breathing was labored. "I got a new paint delivery. I think I'm allergic to something in it." His aim for humor fell way short of the mark, pain evident in every word.

"Call nine-one-one," I barked out, not taking my eyes off of Toady as I knelt next to him on the paint-splattered floor.

I didn't look to see who pulled out their phone as Toady shook his head. "Nah, I'll be fine. I don't need the hospital."

"Shut the fuck up, you're goin'." He visibly blanched. What was his problem?

"It's on the way," Buzz muttered.

"Buzz, get the first aid box. There must be somethin' in there that we can use. The rest of y'all get back to work. It ain't a fucking circus we're runnin' here." That got several grunts and a couple of curious stares before there was a rustle of plastic as guys went back to whatever they'd been doing.

"Here you go." The box was dumped on the floor next to me, and Buzz disappeared. The guy was known for having a weak stomach. Right then, I didn't blame him. Looking at Toad's hand was weirding me out and making my ass clench rather unpleasantly, though I would never have admitted it.

I glanced about for something to put under Toady's head but couldn't see anything. I yanked off my T-shirt and rolled it into a ball. "Lift your head." A catch in my voice had me looking around, hoping the plastic walls would prevent anyone from noticing. With everyone working, my shoulders relaxed a little.

"Now you get naked for me," he said in a low tone laced with a thread of humor.

"Shut up," I growled as I carefully lifted his head and laid it on my shirt, avoiding looking into his sea-blue eyes. Eyes that left me nowhere to hide from what we'd done. For something to do, I opened the box and rooted through the contents. There was so much stuff in there, but I wasn't sure what could be used on the angry-looking hand.

"Unless you got a new hand in there, leave it. I just need a bandage and some pain pills ."

"You need a fuckin' lot more than that."

Toad lifted his hand slowly and looked at it. His lips puffed out and what little color was left in his cheeks bled out. "Fuck, how am I supposed to finish Razor's bike or any of the other jobs I got lined up to do?" The worry was real, and I struggled to keep myself from offering him something that wasn't in my nature, affection.

I knew it had been a mistake, but if I'd listened to myself before, if I'd done what I'd sworn I wouldn't...

The sound of sirens in the distance, which used to make me wonder what we needed to hide, did nothing more than fill me with relief. Toad didn't appear relieved at all as he started to struggle to get up. "I'm fine. I don't need the hospital." He sounded anything but convincing as he swayed.

"Stop with the stupid. I ain't got time for this bullshit." I cuffed the back of his head hard enough that his eyes narrowed on me.

"It ain't fucking stupid, and you're only the boss of me at work, you made that clear," he hissed through clenched teeth, color returning to his cheeks.

The flood of relief was tempered by how hard it was to stop them from saying stupid shit back to him. Heavy, booted feet alerted me to the paramedics, and I glanced up to watch the woman with the guy open and shut her mouth twice as she lifted the plastic. She was pretty, with dark hair and a full figure that a man could get a grip of.

"What you lookin' at? He needs help." I stood and towered over the pair, knowing I made an intimidating sight. Tall, bald, and tattooed with a large naked chest, yeah, that might make someone look twice, but I wasn't interested in that, only in them doing something to help Toad.

"Yes, erm, what happened here?" the guy questioned, gaining his bearings a lot quicker than the woman, who continued to stare at me like she was in some sort of trance. The members of Dark Angels were well known in Bell County, but members tended to avoid hospitals as they asked too many questions.

Even my hard stare didn't seem to work on the woman as I answered the guy before Toad could say a word. "Toad was using new paint, he got some on his hand, and now it's doubled in size and blistered."

The guy nodded before lowering the bag he held to his feet, then crouching down next to Toad.

Toad got a defiant look as he watched the guy pull out a spray bottle and what looked like a large clear plastic bag. "I don't need to go to the hospital." It seemed he had that comment on repeat.

"Don't listen to his shit," I said to the guy as curls of dread wormed their way through me when the woman persisted in gawking. It was growing old real quick. I hated females staring at me, especially the way she was. It made me uneasy since I was sure my brothers thought I should do something about her obvious attraction.

"Let me have a look, determine the extent of what appears to be a nasty burn." The guy gently took hold of Toad's injured hand. The reaction I had to the sight of his tanned hands touching Toad was instant, and I gritted my teeth together to prevent any words from tumbling out of my mouth.

The paramedic shifted his gaze from the hand he held to Toad's face, giving him a sympathetic smile. "I'm sorry, buddy. I think this will need to be surgically cleaned to get all the paint off your skin and out of these blisters."

"Fuck!" he complained, his eyes shutting as his shoulders drooped.

"Can you go grab the chair?" the guy asked the woman, who nodded and spun on her heel.

She got no more than three steps when Toad said, "I'll fucking walk. I haven't lost the use of my legs."

He sounded pissed, and that was way better than defeated. I went to put a hand under his arm to help, and he shook it off. "I can manage." Pain sliced at my heart that I refused to acknowledge. I dropped my hand and watched as he heaved himself to his feet. He swayed, and my hands clenched into fists to stop from reaching out again.

"I'll follow on my bike."

"I don't need no fucking babysitter," he snapped, then staggered through the plastic the woman had lifted toward the open doors as if he'd had too much liquor.

"I never said you did, but you'll fucking need someone to fill out the insurance paperwork. And since you damaged your right hand, it ain't gonna be you," I called after him. His uninjured hand raised in a *whatever* move before he disappeared out of sight.

"Buzz, clean up this shit and call Linc, and let him know what's gone down." With that, I picked up my T-shirt. There were smears of paint on it from where it had been on the ground. I still slipped it back on after brushing at it. The scent of Toady's shampoo mixed with the paint made it hard to concentrate. I went into the office to grab keys and my wallet with the business insurance details.

On my bike five minutes later, I watched the ambulance pull out of the large parking lot in front of the auto shop. I started my engine, slipped on my sunglasses, and zipped out into the traffic to follow. The warm Texas sun heated the skin on my arms, reminding me I'd forgotten my jacket.

Now I had a moment to think, my head started to run through how opposed Toad had been to going to the hospital. Was he scared of hospitals? It was a possibility. Everyone had some fear of something, but it seemed odd that he'd been adamant he wasn't going, especially with his hand so fucked up. He'd mentioned the delay in what he was working on. Was that it? Was it just that he was worried for the business, for his reputation? It had been growing over the past six months with each new custom paint job he did. That side of the business had boomed since he'd come to work for us. Was it simply that?

Something nagged like a bitch and wouldn't let go that it was something else. My gut was seldom wrong. Ears buzzing at the crazy rate of my heart, I took the turn and followed the signs for the hospital parking lot.

Was this really my problem?

The easy answer was no. But there wasn't anything easy about what I felt for the man who had somehow taken up residence like a vagrant, refusing to leave my thoughts. I stopped and flipped down the stand while switching off the engine.

My gaze narrowed on the ambulance parked outside the ER as the doors opened, and the man I'd fucked two months ago appeared on a stretcher. His good arm lay across his eyes, covering them as his lips moved. Too far away to figure out what he was saying, my stomach nosedived. The fucker looked so vulnerable that it hit dead center in a place it had no business aiming for.

What the fuck was I supposed to do with all these feels? I rubbed at my chest as I swung my leg over the bike. Resigned that, whatever was going on with me, I wasn't going to find the answer today or possibly any day soon.

Chapter 2

TOAD

The pain was messing with my head. It had to be because I was out of my mind, agreeing to this madness. I hissed out a breath as the door opened and the two paramedics got busy.

"The drugs I gave you should start to kick in soon," the guy said as the stretcher I was lying on was moved to the open doors.

I laid my good arm over my eyes, praying that no one would see me. Up to now, I'd kept my head down and avoided hospitals. *Five years.*

Would they still be looking for me? I didn't bother to answer my own stupid question because I knew the answer was yes. "Maybe you could just let me off here. I don't need to go in there," I muttered through gritted teeth as the bed jerked and pain shot through my arm and hand.

"You need medical attention," the woman stated in a no-nonsense tone I was sure she probably used on kids.

The muggy heat was oppressive for the few seconds it took for them to wheel me into the ER department as I clamped my lips together. I refused to look about to see if Sid was there, watching with those dark fucking impregnable eyes of his.

Conversations continued around me as I focused on breathing and not letting the panic well inside me. Someone asked for my name. "Toad," I answered.

"Sir, I need your real name."

There was a commotion and the sound of raised voices before I heard the thud of booted feet approaching. My heart fluttered in my chest as I kept the arm over my face.

"Where is he?" Sid asked in a menacing tone.

"As I explained, only next of kin are allowed back through here," a female argued back.

"I am his fucking family. He's my brother."

I was learning to hate those words. "It's fine. Let him come in," I muttered.

"See, it's fucking fine."

This time his voice sounded much closer, and I shifted my arm to peer up. Sid looked fit to murder someone. Intimidating. The word was made for the man glaring at anyone who dared to challenge him.

The petite redhead matching him glare for glare had some balls, that was for sure. I'd seen men piss themselves when that look was aimed at them.

A man in scrubs stepped around the curtain. He was tall, with dark attractive features, and wore his authority like a coat. In the past, he'd have been exactly what I was attracted to. But that was before one man had ruined me.

"What's going on here? This is a hospital with sick patients, not a place to have a brawl," the guy drawled in a deep southern accent.

My guts clenched, and I gave him my full attention. How old was he? Could he have come from the same area as my family?

"We ain't brawling, as you can see unless you're fuckin' blind." Sid pointed to the tiny redhead, "She was bein'...obstructive."

I barked out a laugh at Sid's effort to tone down his language, then regretted it as it jolted my arm. "When are the pain meds supposed to fuckin' work?" I gritted out.

At this, the guy looked at me and then at the paramedics who were still there. "What did you give him?"

The conversation continued, but I didn't hear much of it as it was too much effort to concentrate. Unsure how much time passed before gentle fingers touched my arm, I jerked and cussed up a storm.

"Sorry, we're getting you something a little stronger to help with the pain. I'm Dr. Gill, one of the ER doctors. Can you talk me through what happened?"

"He got paint on his hand. That's what happened," Sid answered for me.

It was a close call when my first reaction was to lift my right hand and give Sid a message he'd understand. "I suffer from allergies, and there must have been somethin' in the paint," I added, not looking at Sid.

"Has it been this severe before?" Dr. Gill's touch was gentle as he turned my hand left and right.

"Once, they had to stick a tube down my throat to help with my breathin'." As I shared that information, there was a sharply indrawn breath from the man who was standing way too close for my peace of mind.

Dr. Gill ignored Sid and continued to ask me several more questions before a woman returned with what I hoped were drugs. I needed them to help stop me from crying because, right then, I couldn't be sure I wasn't going to start. I'd been involved in my share of fights, taking several hard beatings over the years, but my hand was kicking my ass right then. I didn't want to show any weakness in from of Sid. Not now, not ever.

"Can you leave?" I gritted out while the doc was still talking. He glanced at me, and I nodded toward Sid. "Him, not you."

"Ain't happenin'," was Sid's only response as his arms crossed over his impressive chest and

32

distracted me in ways I didn't want or need. The man had made it clear: one lapse in judgment was one too many.

"If he wants you to leave, then I'd suggest you do so." Dr. Gill didn't even look in Sid's direction, but I was a sadist and did.

Fury I'd witness unleashed on others was there sparking in his eyes. His face a mask of meanness. "You deaf? 'Cause, you damn well must be if I'm havin' to repeat myself. *Ain't happenin'*."

The doc swung his gaze to Sid, seemingly unconcerned about the threat in Sid's voice. I couldn't see the doc's expression when Sid raised one eyebrow and gave the guy a feral smile. The air hummed with tension to the point it distracted from the pain in my arm as I readied myself to get up and get between these two men. The woman looked disgruntled but said nothing as she injected the substance into the thing the paramedics had stuck in my good hand in the ambulance.

"Not deaf, just don't take any bullshit from anyone," Dr. Gill replied in a neutral tone. Yet his posture was anything but as he stood tall, turning to face Sid fully, and it was then I noticed he was the same height as Sid. Around six-four was my best guess.

"Then get on with what you're paid to do."

Whatever the nurse had given me started to take effect as everything inside me began to feel as if I'd downed a fifth of whiskey. "Whatever, someone do something to fix my hand so I can leave," I slurred and shut my eyes to help stop the room from spinning.

That was the last thing I remembered until I woke in an unfamiliar room. I blinked several times as panic flared in my chest. My body felt as if I was pinned to the bed, my right hand was placed in some odd-looking foam, and my left had an IV line attached that went to a machine. Had they found me? What had they done to me? Had they given me...

I shut my stinging eyes and worked to take several deep breaths.

"What's up? You need pain meds?" Sid growled.

I jerked, and my eyes opened to scan the room. There was Sid, looking like he'd just woken up. His normally smooth chin had scruff on it, and his clothes looked like he'd slept in them. "How long..." I swallowed, doing my best to keep the panic at bay, "have I been here?" Had I given them my name? Had they looked for my family?

Sid rubbed at his face. "Two days. The stuff they gave you downstairs knocked you out. The doc, after examining your hand, had to get a plastic surgeon to look at it." His brow furrowed. "You got a little freaked out when you woke, so they sedated you to clean and bandage your hand."

The layer of drugs fogging my brain wouldn't let me remember. Heart hammering against my ribs, I eyed Sid. "Freaked out?"

"You lashed out with your damaged hand and started shouting some shit about not letting them take you." He looked weary as he sat on the edge of the hospital bed. "You wanna tell me what that was about?"

Glad the lighting in the room was dim enough to keep the flush of heat hidden, I shook my head. "No clue, was probably the drugs they gave me." Even to my own ears, I sounded unconvincing, and the deep, grim lines around Sid's mouth said the same.

His powerful shoulders lifted. "If you say so."

Did he sound disappointed? Nah, he'd been clear. He wasn't interested in more than one fuck. *He's your club brother; that's why he's worried.* That didn't help.

I shut my eyes to block out the other man, who continued to stare at me. It was then it dawned on me what he had said, and my eyes slit open. "You're wearin' the same clothes. Have you been here for the two days?"

The worry about my name was forgotten as he shifted on the bed. His gaze moved from me to the window, where he showed a little too much interest considering it had blinds covering it. What was that about?

The silence lengthened as tension crept through me while I tried to figure out what his actions indicated. "Linc wanted someone to stay, make sure you were okay," he finally answered, his gaze firmly fixed on the window.

I laughed, but it lacked any humor. "Thanks, but as you can see, I'm fine. You can go." I blocked him out, but the pain in my heavily bandaged hand kept me awake.

There was the sound of a buzzer, and a few seconds later, the door opened and bright light flooded the room. "You need something, Sid?" The woman sounded way too flirty as I glanced at the sweet-looking blonde who was doing this fluttery thing with her eyelashes.

"Toad needs somethin' for the pain."

She stepped into the room and came to the bed, her hips swaying sexily. I gritted my teeth when I noticed that Sid gave her one of his half-smiles. "You're finally awake. Let me call the doctor and let him know. Then I'll bring you something to help with the pain."

When she left the room seconds later, I glanced at Sid. "Did you give them my name?"

His brows rode up his forehead, but it was too late to keep the fear hidden. "Yeah, they needed it for the insurance."

He hadn't finished talking before I was yanking at the needle in my arm, shifting to the edge of the bed.

"What the fuck are you doin'?"

"Leaving," I muttered as I swayed for a second when I stood. I sucked in a steadying breath then looked about for my clothes. Blood trickled from where the needle had been in my arm onto the gown I wore, but that was the least of my worries.

"Get the fuck back in the bed," Sid growled as he came around to the other side of the bed, his face set in a familiar scowl.

"No, ain't happening. Where are my clothes?"

"What's this about? Fucking tell me."

The concern stopped me for a brief second until I recalled his behavior over the last two months. "None of your fuckin' business." With that, I went to the cabinet and dragged open the door. My clothes were there, and I grabbed them.

A strong hand landed on my left arm. "Tell me."

I swung around and gritted my teeth, my jaw flexing with the effort not to cry out with the renewed pain flowing through me at the sudden movement. "You made it clear two months ago. Nothin' personal. Now back the fuck up and let me get dressed." I might not be as strong as him, but I'd fight him if I needed to. Right then, my only priority was getting out.

Whatever he saw on my face, he gave a nod and took a step back. "I'll drop you off at home." He swung around and exited the door. I sagged against the nearest wall, all my energy gone.

It was for the best. It had to be.

Chapter 3

SID

"**W**hat's chewin' your ass?" Linc rasped as he glanced up from the design he was working on.

It always amazed me how he could create such beauty on paper first before working on someone's body. I shook my head, "Nothin'." *Or nothing I wanted to talk about right then*. I couldn't get my head on straight, so it was best to keep quiet.

"Don't give me that bullshit. I've had Ram and Buzz complain' you got something stuck where the sun don't shine. Fuck's sake, spit it out." He didn't look back up from what he was doing, making it a damn sight easier for me, whether he realized it or not.

"Toad...there's somethin' goin' on with him."

Linc placed his pen down carefully and, this time, met my worried stare. "Somethin' connected to the rat bastards?"

"Nope, not that he didn't fight hard when shit went down, but this is something else." I ran a hand over my bald head and got up with the beer I'd grabbed from Linc's fridge when I'd arrived minutes earlier, walking to the door that led onto the porch. I'd come on the pretense of talking about the auto shop. I'd fooled no one. Linc wasn't an idiot, but he also wasn't one to push.

"Then, what? Is it work? We'd agreed to pay him while he's out of action." Linc sounded frustrated and more than a little pissed. That was usual for him, so I didn't take offense.

"Poppy, Poppy, where are ya?" River shouted at the top of her lungs before the sound of tiny feet hit the wooden stairs.

Linc never got the chance to reply as River burst through the door with Mason right behind her, looking like he'd been in a wind tunnel.

My brows rose at the normally immaculate man. "Where you've been?" I pointed with the hand holding the bottle at his head. "You look a little...disheveled," I added at the end when Linc gave me a stern warning stare. The man was protective of Mason and wouldn't let anyone give him shit. It'd been jarring to watch Linc fall for his lawyer and stick two fingers up at anyone who showed too much interest.

There were no secrets between us. I'd always known Linc was gay as he knew I was. We just didn't talk about that crap, ever. That was until Mason appeared on the scene. Now, well, I wasn't sure how that was going to work out. It was still early days, but it seemed that Mason was all but living with Linc.

Mason ran his hand through his hair, and River giggled. "We's been sailing on the lake."

Linc barked out a laugh. "Sailing?"

"Yes, sailing. It was fun, wasn't it, River?" Mason ran a gentle hand down River's dark hair and smiled at her, full of love. It touched something deep inside me. River had a special place in my heart, and I'd cut the legs off anyone that hurt her. I'd spent a lot of time helping Linc in the beginning when her mamma died. It had been downright scary, yet the little girl had wormed her way into my heart.

"It was. Next time, Poppy, you's coming with us."

His brows arched. "I'll pass, Spirit."

Her hands went to her hips and her chin jutted out much the same way Linc's did when he got stubborn. "Poppy, you's promised. I didn't forget."

I bit the inside of my cheek to keep the smile from crossing my face when Linc looked resigned.

"I'll be gentle on you." Mason chuckled.

"Fu—"

"Poppy, you's know the rules," River said before Linc could finish.

The laughter was out this time, and I ignored the blistering glare Linc sent my way. I finished the beer and walked over to the recycling bin, dropping it inside. "You're busy. I'll catch you tomorrow at the clubhouse." The next planned meeting was the following day to talk about the changes that were coming.

Linc's hand rose. "We haven't finished."

"We have, for now." I bent and hugged River when she raised her arms to me.

"Sid, you gonna come and read me a story soon? You's do such a good job with the voices."

There was a choked cough that I thought came from Mason, but I didn't look up as I nodded. "I'll come over next week." I laid a quick kiss on her nose and stood, ignoring the other two men as I walked to the door.

"Bring the file with you tomorrow," Linc called after me.

I raised a hand to acknowledge I'd heard and understood what he meant before heading out into the hallway, down the stairs, and exiting through the front door. I inhaled the warm evening scent that was purely Texas as I strode to my hog parked in the drive. I glanced about the quiet neighborhood and sighed.

When Linc had decided to change things, he hadn't gone and done it by any half measures. Once he'd become legal guardian to his niece, he'd made some drastic changes. Buying this huge house and shifting his business into a suburban neighborhood had been a risk, and it had paid off. Changing the dealings at the auto shop was another risk. One I'd argued about initially until Linc had told me to shut up. I had, and he'd proven me wrong. With some advertisement, the business had recouped the losses we'd made from going legit.

The small sideline I'd had on the high end, stolen parts for specific cars, had been a loss. But Linc had signed over a percentage of the business, making up for his decision. It had proven less stressful and equally as profitable. I'd eaten crow over that. Linc wasn't one to shove stuff in your face, so we'd let it be.

The only issue was the old crew, members that had been recruited by Linc's granddaddy. They hadn't taken the changes lightly.

Understatement! Who sets up the president of their club on charges of rape?

I worked to shove what had gone down with Doddie, Ned, Stevie, and Ricky, along with some of the newer members of Dark Angels, to the back of my mind. Where I'd been shoving Toad for the last week. The guy wasn't answering his door or messages, and he was ignoring my phone calls.

I didn't have a clue if he was all right since I'd dropped him off at home the week before. He'd looked like shit, and the hospital had been none too happy he'd left against medical advice. But no amount of talking had made him change his mind. I'd sent Buzz round to see him this morning, and he hadn't gotten any further than me. The club meeting tomorrow was mandatory for all members, and since Toad had only recently got his patch, it wouldn't look good if he didn't attend. I'd sent a message saying just that. It had been read, but there'd been no reply, just like the others.

On my bike, I glanced down at my black tank. I'd mentioned to Linc about getting Toad to do a paint job on it. At the time I'd realized my mistake, my relationship with my bike was well known. I fucking loved the thing. It was the first thing I'd bought myself when I'd gotten my share of the profits from a lucrative side chop-shop job we'd done.

The Harley was a rare beast and a thing of beauty. I had a garage built at the back of the auto shop to keep it. Mentioning I would let the other man touch it revealed far more than I'd intended. Again, Linc didn't pry into anyone else's business unless directly connected to the club, so he'd let it be, and I hadn't mentioned it again. Was that why I hadn't booked the job with Toad? Was I worried about what my brothers would think?

It was a hard call.

I zipped down the road, my sunglasses protecting my eyes from the low-lying sun as I headed in the direction of where my thoughts had been nagging me. Several minutes later, I pulled up outside Toad's apartment block. The street was quiet, ensuring Toad would have heard my bike coming.

I glanced up at the top floor, and there in the window was Toad. I couldn't make out his features, but his shoulders sagged in defeat. I swung my leg off the bike and walked to the front door. I didn't press Toad's bell. I rang the three others, hoping someone would just buzz me in.

When the lock buzzed a second later, I pushed into the building and walked up the four flights of stairs. Outside Toad's apartment, I hammered on the door. "Let me in," I growled.

I waited for a minute before I hammered again. "I ain't leavin'."

A few seconds later, there was the sound of chains and a lock disengaging before Toad appeared. His face was thinner, there were dark circles around his sunken eyes, and the scent of unwashed clothes and skin curled my nose. I eyed him, and the worry that had been my constant friend since I'd left him berated me. Why had I left?

His dominant hand wrapped in thick bandages was the only answer I needed as to why the guy was in this state. Or was it? His weird behavior in the hospital was still unexplained. I swallowed the sigh of frustration and anger as I shoved past him, not saying anything. Three steps into the apartment, and my heart rate sped up. The place was a disaster zone. He looked as if he'd hunkered down on the couch and hadn't moved. A thick rug lay in a big heap at the end of the couch. There were cups and plates scattered about on both the table and floor with dried food on them.

This had to stop.

Before I realized my intention, I checked out the other doors to find which one was his bedroom.

"What you doin'?" His voice sounded rusty, like he hadn't used it in a while.

"Packin' a bag. You're comin' back to mine." I ground out, barely keeping the anger under control as I started to pull open drawers. Yanking out what looked clean, I threw it on the bed.

Toad stood in the doorway, his features set in a stubborn mask I'd seen a time or two. "Not happenin'."

"It is, even if I have to bodily carry you out of here." I met his stare with a hard one of my own as I pointed at him. "You're a fuckin' mess. You need a damn keeper. When's your appointment at the hospital to get the bandage changed?"

"None of your damn business." His tone was petulant.

The anger at what he was doing to himself wouldn't soften as I stalked toward him, taking hold of the top of his arms in a punishing grip to shake him. "You're my brother. I'm your boss. Those two things right there say it's my damn business." I gave him another hard shake with how much I wanted to say he meant something more to me. Letting out my anger was a better alternative right then because I struggled to keep my thoughts to myself when I was mad.

"Let go of me," he rasped, his eyes firing back anger to match my own.

"No. What you gonna do about it?" I laughed, then saw my mistake when he distracted me by moving his injured arm while bringing up his knee and connecting it hard with my balls.

They lodged somewhere up in my throat as my eyes watered, and I struggled to keep a hold of him with my need to rub at my now throbbing nuts. I wheezed out a breath. "Motherfucker."

"Let go." His whole body was primed for a fight. I could see it, feel it in the tension rolling off him.

My heart rate kicked up several levels, and I wasn't sure if it was anger or desire. Right then, it was a close call. The night we'd fucked, Toad had made it clear he wasn't going to be the one on the receiving end. The way he was behaving right now, my body was reacting to the aggressive show, and I wasn't happy with the need to bend over and let him fuck me into next week.

I closed my eyes and willed the images away while sucking in several shaky breaths. I dropped my hands and took a step back as I stared into the stormy gaze. "You're comin' with me. I ain't arguing about this. You need help, take it." The sliver of desperation in my voice set my teeth on edge.

Toad stood for several more seconds, staring at me like he was seeing me for the first time.

He shook his head, and as I opened my mouth to say something, he started speaking, "A week, I'll give you a week." With that, he walked on stiff legs to the bed and one-handed pawed through what I'd pulled out.

The seconds ticked by as I went to the closet to search for a bag that could slip over his shoulders. There was no way I was heading back for the work truck to collect him. I had a feeling that if he was given a chance, he'd change his mind. Once we were on the street, the hoodie, I'd thought was odd in the heat, was pulled up over his head as he kept his gaze down.

Thoughts that made no sense started to ping around my head. Was he scared and hiding? If so, from what? Or who? I slung my leg over my hog and waited for him to sit behind me. The thoughts fled as his body pressed up against mine. The stale scent was there, but so was his familiar fragrance, and my groin reacted as it always did. Under my breath, I cursed as he nestled his pelvis against my ass and his left hand circled my waist and held on. His palm felt perfect as it settled against my thin T-shirt.

There's no such fucking thing!

You keep believing that!

Chapter 4

TOAD

The week had been hell. Who the fuck could manage to do anything one-handed? Clearly not me, and I'd given up trying. To add to that, I hadn't been able to sleep for shit. Every time I heard a noise, I'd jerked awake and get up to look outside, expecting to see several cars and guys with a straitjacket come to cart me away.

Life had been hell, then Sid had ridden up on his fucking Harley and come to the rescue when my defenses were at an all-time low. The urge to just give in to him had been tempered with the whole *I'm your brother and boss*. Those were not the words I wanted to hear from him. Fuck no, I'd wanted him to beg because he wanted me. The fact I'd kneed him in the nuts and was still breathing had to say something about his feelings, right? Or was he just feeling sorry for me?

A shudder ran through me as I clung a little tighter to him, needing for a second to believe it wasn't pity he felt or brotherhood. I'd always been a dreamer. Wasn't that why I was here, getting lost in a place my family would never think of? It was why I'd applied to become a prospect for Dark Angels, needing to feel a part of something where folks stood up for me and didn't judge me for my choices in life.

The sob nearly choked me, and Sid's large body stiffened as if he felt it. His hand touched mine, and I laid my head on his back for several seconds. His hand moved as we approached the intersection to turn off into the industrial area where the auto shop was located.

The empty lot in front was a relief as Sid headed around the back. He was silent as he switched off the engine and waited for me to get off first. The bag on my back shifted, reminding me what was about to happen. As I eyed the door leading to his apartment above the auto shop, I had a moment of panic. Was I potentially bringing trouble to Sid's door?

Even with his insistence, I couldn't talk myself out of the reality that if shit went down here, it would be my fault because Sid was clueless about my past.

I kicked at the ground as I watched him unlock the building he stored his bike in. It brought back memories of the night we'd come here to fuck. He'd left his bike out front, and at the time, I'd wondered why. Later I realized he'd done it so he had an excuse to get me out of his bed and out the door before anyone could see us.

He was back two minutes later, swinging the keys in his hand. "You eaten?"

I shook my head. I'd lived on takeout because I hadn't figured out how to cook without the use of my right hand. Every time I tried to do something, I'd instantly been reminded by pain that I had an injured hand that didn't want me doing anything with it.

I'd stopped changing my clothes and showering with how hard everything was to do with only one hand to help me. It was pathetic. I was pathetic.

He held the door open and moved to let me pass. I walked up the stairs much as I had months earlier, but with one big difference, he wasn't interested in fucking this time. Now he was my babysitter. I sighed. What a fucking come down.

Silence remained between us as he led me into the apartment that, this time, was clean and tidy. The space was large and open, the living space was all one. The kitchen wasn't big and was tucked into the far corner of the room. There was a large wooden table that he'd used to separate the spaces. The couches were large and leather and pushed against the wall at the other end of the room and faced a large flat-screen TV that hung suspended on the wall. There was a large leather armchair sitting in front of it and a small table off to the side. There were a couple of rugs on the wooden floor. There weren't any knickknacks anywhere. The only picture on the wall above the couch was of Sid's bike. I was aware that Linc had commissioned it from a local artist when Sid stepped up as his second in the club.

The brothers were a chatty bunch. I often sat and listened to them talk about stuff, and they often forgot I was there. I'd learned from a very young age to try and blend in with the furniture.

"Follow me," Sid growled, pulling me from my observations.

He walked down the hallway leading to where I knew was his bedroom. He went past his door to the one next to his and shoved it open, nodding. "It's clean. A woman makes sure it is in case I have any visitors."

Jealousy swirled around my guts, churning them at who would be his visitors. I wasn't aware he had any family, other than those he chose to call brother. "Thanks," I muttered as I stepped around him and into the room. It was large and spacious, done in gray and black, much like the rest of the apartment. It suited the stoic man.

The bed was big and looked comfy. There was a door leading off to what I suspected was a bathroom. I poked my head in and was proven right. I eyed the enclosed shower stall then looked back at Sid. "I can't shower," I raised my injured hand, "'cause I'm struggling to do anything with this."

A dark color flared over Sid's cheekbones as his face gave nothing else away about what he was thinking. "I'll help you. You stink and need a wash."

"Thanks," I muttered again, doing my best not to cringe at the truth of what he'd said. I did stink. It was enough to turn a guy off, I was sure.

"I'll sort something to eat, then give you a hand." He was gone before I could say anything else. I perched on the edge of the bed and shrugged off the bag. This was a bad fucking idea. The worst.

I glanced at my lap. "Don't go getting any fuckin' ideas."

Realizing what I was doing, I got up and unpacked slowly. The closet was empty but full of hangers. It took longer than it should, trying to hang shit up while the hanger was tucked under my arm pit. I was sweating and out of sorts by the time Sid shouted that the food was ready.

The last of the hangers was thrown on the bed as I stomped into the hall. I stopped for a second at the heavenly scent that greeted me. Had he cooked? I walked slowly into the living room to see Sid placing two full plates of fried chicken, baked potato, coleslaw, and corn on the cob. Sitting on a plate in the middle of the table were butter and sour cream.

My stomach growled loudly. A blush rode up my neck as Sid's lips twitched into a familiar half-smile. "Sit, eat."

I followed his command because my stomach was suddenly awake and raring to go. I eyed the chicken and picked it up with my left hand, not even attempting to cut it. Sid sat and said nothing as he took my plate and put just the right amount of butter and sour cream on my potato before cutting it into bites I could easily eat. It was such an intimate thing to do that I couldn't take my eyes off of him.

The hard outer shell many didn't see past was there, but so was the caring nature that I'd spent months discovering as I'd watched him. The man had so many hidden depths, one being the shame he felt for being gay. I understood it more than he'd ever know. It was why he wasn't into repeats; I was positive. He didn't want attachments that meant he'd have to acknowledge who he really was. It was fucking sad. That had to be a lonely existence, and I should know, I was the king of those.

Chapter 5

SID

The shower stall was big enough for me to get in with Toad, but I wasn't sure I was ready for that level of intimacy. The meal the night before was bad enough, and straight after, Toad had gone off to his room. I didn't offer to help him take off his clothes or do anything else that might involve him being naked in front of me.

All night I'd stewed in my own damn juice, knowing Toad couldn't have showered before he went to bed. So here I was, staring at the shower, while the man in question lay in bed sleeping like the dead. He hadn't stirred when I'd come in five minutes ago. Nothing, not even a twitch. His face was buried in the pillow, and he still wore the top he'd had on last night. His lower body was covered with a sheet, and it was clear he'd removed his jeans. Had he taken off his underwear?

My hand lowered to my cock, and I repositioned myself, my gaze on Toad.

"I didn't take you for a peeper," Toad said in a muffled, sleep-roughened voice. His face remained in the pillow.

The hand that had been on my cock dropped to my side while the heat of embarrassment crawled up my neck. "Peeper? Don't they look through a damn window?"

He shifted and glanced sideways at me through slitted eyes. "Fuck knows, but standing there sayin' nothing and staring isn't the way to wake someone up." He winced as he moved to sit, and the sheet pooled around his lap. His hair was stuck up all over the place. He looked...too fucking sexy for his own good.

It was far more difficult to keep my eyes on his face. "I came to check out the shower." Why the fuck did I say that?

"Why? You plannin' on helpin' me?" He smirked.

"You stink. That bed probably stinks too now." I pointed out, trying to hide my discomfort and shield my thoughts.

The show he made of sniffing his top would have been funny if not for the way his nose curled up. "Yeah, I do." He eyed his bandaged hand. "This has made me pretty useless." Although the dark circles under his eyes were less obvious, the deep lines around his mouth hadn't lessened.

It took all my will not to walk to the bed to offer...not happening.

"Get up. I'll help cause you ain't stinkin' up my home." The gruffness got Toad to tilt his head to the side, and his eyes narrowed on me.

"You just wanna see me naked," he joked, a smile tugging at his lips.

"Been there done that, I don't do seconds."

"You missed out on sloppy seconds. What are we, in a remake of fucking *Grease*?"

"Fuck off." I struggled not to laugh as his smile increased in wattage, nearly blinding me.

"You should do that more often."

I frowned. "Do what?"

"Smile. It transforms your whole face."

He appeared to be serious, and I had no answer to that. Smiling was never my thing, not when there was so little to smile about with my lonely existence. *Get over yourself.*

"Get up. I'll help you shower before I head down to the shop." I didn't wait for his reply and swung back around to go into the bathroom.

There was the sound of movement as I stripped off my T-shirt and left on the sweatpants I'd slipped on. The water was warm by the time Toad appeared in the doorway with some sort of plastic thing over his hand and fuck all else. His soft cock hung between his legs. Just as before, the hair there was trimmed so short it was impossible to grip it. My fingers twitched with the memory of how it had felt against my skin.

57

I swallowed and looked at his face, but his gaze lingered on my tattoo. The serpent that finished on my skull started at my chest. The tail was wrapped around my upper body. Each scale could be clearly seen, and when I moved my muscles, it looked like the snake was moving. Linc had outdone himself. The colors were bold, and the eyes that sat on the side of my skull glowed in the dark.

"A picture lasts longer," I muttered when he continued to stand there not moving.

"I know, but it wouldn't do your body justice. Take my word for it." His sexy rasp didn't help what was happening inside my sweatpants.

"Shower," I twisted, opened the door, and made room for him to walk past without touching me. But he made sure his body brushed mine. The stale scent wasn't as bad without the clothes.

He stepped into the warm water, his right arm held out to the side as he groaned. "Fuck, that feels so good."

Water sluiced down his far too thin frame as he shut his eyes and tilted his head back. The water darkened the hair that touched his shoulders. His nipples pebbled and his cock started to plump.

A feeling of desperation ran through me as I grabbed for the shower gel and poured a liberal amount on my hands. I eyed the man in front of me like he might bite as I stepped fully into the stall.

His eyes glittered as they opened, his tongue licking at the water droplets clinging to his lips. The invitation in his eyes was hard to resist as I recalled the chemistry between us. Toad's body was a sin, and he knew how to use every inch to wring out my pleasure.

His left hand stroked down his body and took hold of his cock. He caressed it firmly from base to tip until a bead of precum gathered on the tip. It hung suspended for several seconds before it dripped to the tiled floor. I bit the inside of my cheek to stop the moan of displeasure from revealing how much I wanted to chase his essence to taste him.

"I thought you were going to help me?" His voice was low and seductive.

Inhaling the steaming air, I stood taller and willed my hands to not shake as I met the other man's challenge. Slowly I rubbed my hands together before starting at his shoulders. I stroked over his silky skin that covered hard muscles.

His eyelids fluttered closed, his hand continuing to stroke his cock. Gently I washed his right arm to where the bag was, avoiding going too close to the seal. I left his other arm, instead working my soapy hands over his pecs and down to his navel. His stomach rippled under my touch, and he made a small whimpering sound. His eyes remained closed, which I was thankful for because the way my sweatpants were tented made it obvious how much I was enjoying the freedom to touch him. Neither of us spoke as I moved to go behind him. The air felt thick and heavy against my skin—the intimacy of the act not lost on me. My heart repeatedly flipped as I massaged his back after getting more shower gel. The scent of fresh lemons filled the stall.

I took my time before I got down on my knees behind him and soaped his legs. The hair was fine and soft. As my hand worked between his thighs, they quivered. The sound of him jacking his cock became the only thing I could concentrate on as I parted his ass cheeks, spreading them to slip my slick fingers over the puckered flesh. His hips rocked slightly, but he didn't do anything else to encourage me to go further.

After torturing myself with the sight of his ass, I stood and moved around the front of him again. His heavy-lidded gaze met mine, and I was held transfixed as he let out a guttural groan, cum spurting out on the floor between us.

Silently I reached for him, and his hand dropped away as I stroked him with soapy fingers, prolonging his orgasm. His chest rose and fell rapidly, his eyes held mine, and in them, I saw things I didn't want to acknowledge that had been there ever since I'd broken my own rule and brought him home with me.

"We can't do this," I gritted out even as I continued to touch him, unwilling to stop when I was desperate to...

"We are."

Those two words derailed my thoughts, and I struggled to stay in the shower. I finished washing him, then helped him dry before I dripped my way back to my own bedroom and shut the door. Leaning against it, I stared at the room. It was the only one in the apartment that truly reflected who I was. The bookcases I'd made with bits of old sleepers were built into the far wall next to the bed. There were thousands of books I'd bought over the years. The range was broad to meet my many moods when I was alone and needed to lose myself.

There was a couple of pictures on the opposite wall that River had made for me. The large set of drawers was the only surface that held several trinkets I'd collected. They were all Harley-related. I was a little obsessed.

Toad, when he'd seen my room, hadn't focused on the huge bed in the middle of the room but on my things. I rubbed at my face, noticing the water pooling at my feet. I trudged through to my bathroom, stripping before I got into the shower. Ignoring my own arousal, I washed quickly, keeping my mind empty.

It was way harder than I'd admit. By the time I was dressed and had cleaned up the mess on the floor, I was running late. Going to the kitchen, there was no sign of Toad. I put on the coffee pot and stuck four slices of bread in the toaster. I wolfed down the food and drank a cup of coffee. A sigh of defeat escaped as I made more toast and placed that with coffee on the one tray I'd bought.

Outside Toad's room, I knocked once before stomping in. Toad was leaning at an awkward angle against the wall, trying to use his left hand to tug up his jeans.

I dumped the tray on the bed and walked to him. "Here." I placed his hand on my shoulder and tugged up his jeans. The scent of lemon and the warmth of his body shrouded me, and my none-too-happy cock bucked.

"Thanks," Toad whispered next to my ear, his lips brushing against the rim.

A full-body shiver followed, and I bit back the moan as I removed his hand and stepped back. I stared at him for long seconds, my guts twisting into knots. "I'll be back at lunchtime to feed you." With that, I spun on my heel and left before I completely lost all sense of reason.

Chapter 6

TOAD

Three days, sixteen hours, and thirty-two minutes, that was how long I'd been in Sid's home, and I'd had countless jerk-off sessions to keep myself from doing the one thing the other man didn't seem to want from me, fucking. His eyes begged for it, but the off-limits sign he kept throwing up was too obvious for me to break.

Boundaries I respected, I understood what it was like to have those choices taken away from me, and I'd never do that to Sid. No matter how fucking difficult it was to have him wash me or do all the other things he felt I needed done for me.

The guy spent more time helping me than in the auto shop. He'd even forgone the club meeting when I said I couldn't face it. The pain in my hand could still kick my ass when I overdid it. I hated taking the pain meds they gave me at the hospital because they made me spacey and a little more inclined to crawl all over Sid's gorgeous body.

He didn't have a gym-honed body, far from it. His was hard as a fucking rock from manual labor. Add in all those delicious fucking tattoos that made him irresistible to me, and he was my kryptonite. I wasn't sure how I was going to survive the week we'd agreed to.

I flopped back on the bed, it was comfy, and I didn't have any trouble finding sleep when I lay down. The week of worry before Sid had insisted I come and stay with him had been filled with little to no sleep. I'd more than made up for that over the last few days. I'd slept twelve hours straight, twice, and I was sure I'd be doing the same again tonight. It was a mind fuck to know that I felt a lot safer with Sid next door. I wasn't sure how I would feel when I had to return to my apartment. It was going to be a real hardship, that I knew.

My whole life, I'd never truly felt safe anywhere. My family had made sure of that with their beliefs about what was wrong and right in the world. There was a lot more wrong in their view, and I was definitely sitting in the bad column. I stared up at the ceiling, willing the past out of my head.

They hadn't found me in over five years. Maybe they'd stopped looking? Did I really believe that? My eyes drifted shut as they stung with tears.

There was a knock on the door before Sid's bald head appeared. I sat up, working to keep my emotions in check as I rubbed at my eyes as if I'd been asleep.

When deep lines appeared around his mouth and eyes, I swallowed the mournful sigh. "What?"

"Linc's here. He wants a word."

My stomach did a nice nosedive as I slowly got off the bed. Had someone been nosing about the clubhouse?

Sid remained in the doorway, his gaze never leaving me. "What's up?"

It was there, the wealth of concern I was sure he wasn't aware he was revealing that did crazy things to my heart. "Nothin'," I lied and stepped past him. He didn't stop me, but he followed. The scent of grease and his cologne telling me how close he was to me. My cock plumped, and I started to mix paint colors in my head to distract myself.

Linc was sitting on the larger of the two couches, holding a beer bottle. His face gave nothing away as I walked into the room. "Hey."

His gaze moved to my hand and back to my face. "When's your hospital appointment?"

Not sure why he was leading with that, I answered, "It's on Monday of next week. The doc mentioned somethin' about skin grafts, depending on how it's healing."

A shudder ran through me at the idea of having to go back into the hospital. Sid laid a hand on my shoulder and, for a second, I forgot myself, leaning into his touch. Linc's frown was all it took to remind me of where I was. I shifted and walked away from Sid. He growled low in his throat but said nothing as I took a seat.

There was speculation I didn't often see from Linc as he glanced between Sid and me before he raised a brow in Sid's direction. "Something goin' on here I need to know about?" His voice gave no indication as to what he was thinking.

I kept silent, leaving Sid to answer.

"Nothin' you need to worry about," Sid replied, cutting at my heart regardless of the fact that he'd been honest from the start.

The slow nod Linc gave spoke volumes. The man didn't believe Sid, but he didn't call him out. Instead he indicated with the bottle to Sid. "Sit. I wanna let you know I didn't mention any of the things we were plannin' on discussin' in church the other night. It wasn't the time with both you and Toad not there."

There was no heat as he spoke, so I relaxed back into the padded cushion and listened.

"Sorry, I explained Toad wasn't up for it and since he can't do jack shit for himself..." he shrugged, not adding anything else.

"I get it. Brothers in need are always a priority. The meeting is planned for Tuesday. It seems to fit with Toad's hospital appointment. That leads to me whether we need to be lookin' for another guy to take up some of the slack with Toad out of action for god knows how long."

"What, you lookin' to replace me?" The panic came fast and took hold as I stared wide-eyed at Linc. I'd worked my ass off to get in with Dark Angels, doing every grunt job they gave me to earn my patch, my protection. The job at the auto shop had been the icing on the cake. I'd never gone to art school like I'd wanted, not that these guys knew that. I wouldn't have been able to survive doing artwork without advertising. The distinct style of my work would have been recognized by my family, which made it a hard no for me. So, I'd learned in different auto shops as I'd moved across the counties, getting as far away from my family without using my credit cards or anything that could be traced back to me until I'd gained enough skill to apply for the job at Stone's auto shop. The little town of Belton was miles from where I'd come from, but now it was home, and I didn't want to have to leave.

"We don't replace our brothers. Get real. I'm happy to continue to keep you on the payroll until your hand is fixed. Because you've done your job so fuckin' well building up your paint jobs, I don't want to lose that side of the business before you're able to return."

A wave of heat at the compliment rose, and I glanced away only to look directly at Sid. The pride on his face did funny things to me, leaving me struggling to remain still.

"Do you know anyone who'd be interested?" Sid asked in a gruff voice.

I shook my head. "Not to sound big-headed, but none of the guys I've met have the skill for the delicate work."

Linc chuckled. "Big-headed or not, Sid mentioned you touchin' his pride and joy, that in itself tells me all I need to know about your skill level." He eyed my hand again and sighed. "We'll see what Monday brings. Let's not look for trouble."

He stayed a little longer, but I didn't pay much attention to what they discussed as I ran through all the guys I'd worked with. There were numerous places I'd been as I skipped from one state to the next. I'd been in Austin, in the same bar I'd followed Sid to months before. It was where I'd first seen Sid. The other man hadn't noticed me, but he'd instantly caught my eye. I'd sat in the back of the bar, watching him. That night he'd sat and drunk his beer, finally leaving alone. I'd followed him at a distance. Used to blending into the background, he hadn't noticed me as he'd ridden off on his motorcycle, but the patch on his jacket had me doing a little digging. It hadn't taken much to figure out what biker club he was associated with.

When I'd hit Belton after seeing the job advertised at Stone's, I'd thought for a second it was kismet when it turned out to be the bald-headed, tattoo giant I'd had more than one hot dream about. That was over a year ago, and since then, I'd become his brother and one-time fuck buddy.

The man was complicated and all kinds of fucked up about who he was, but none of that seemed to matter to my heart. It ached, and there was fuck-all I could do about it.

Sid glanced at me with a worried expression as Linc stood. Shit, what had I missed?

"I'll expect you at the club Tuesday, no excuses. Let me know how things go on Monday."

I nodded at Linc. "Will do. I'll also think about anyone who might be able to fill in for me."

"As I said, we'll leave it for now and wait."

I arched my brow, then recalled what he'd said earlier.

Sid walked to the door. "I'll see you out."

Seconds later, they disappeared and left me wondering if Sid had gone down so they could talk freely.

I got up and headed to my room, not wanting to go through the usual awkwardness that had developed between us since the first day I'd pleasured myself in front of Sid. Showers now were a much quicker affair, regretfully. I didn't push, okay I might have pushed a little, but the man was sex on legs. Always there every time I turned around. Wearing a concerned look that left me warm and tingly.

I blew out a breath and flopped back on the bed, careful of my hand. Back to staring up at the ceiling, I counted off the number of hours I had left in Sid's home. Not nearly enough, not anywhere near enough.

Chapter 7

SID

"Yes, I heard you the first time, and as I explained, Toad is out of commission right now, and I have no clue when he'll be able to finish your artwork. You can come and collect your motorcycle anytime you want."

Razor's heavy breathing filled my ear as he made grumbling noises. "How much did he manage to get done?"

The office door was shut, making it impossible to see his bike, and if I was truthful, I hadn't bothered to check what was still left to be done. Toad had well and truly shoved my head up my ass living with me. Every time I turned around, he was there watching me with those big eyes of his.

"Gimme five, and I'll check."

"I don't wanna ride my hog if I'm gonna look like a dweeb."

The guy always looked like a dweeb on his bike, but he was my brother, so I'd never say that to him. I placed the phone on the desk and walked out into the auto shop, heading to the sectioned-off part Toad used. The motorcycle was where it had been when Toad had his accident. On the wall behind the bike was an intricate pattern of skulls and cutthroat razor blades intertwined in a macabre design. The drawing was stunning, even in black and white. When I glanced at the tank, Toad had started with silver for the razor blades and a dark-red shaded to nearly black at the edges where blood dripped down onto the white skulls. One side of the tank was complete, and the other side had yet to be started. In its current state, it still looked mean as fuck.

Had Toad done my design yet? I'd asked a while back for him to come up with a design for my hog, but with cleaning house, I'd forgotten to ask about it again. I tucked the thought away for later and walked back toward my office.

Grease and motor oil were all I could smell as I ignored the men busy working on the several vehicles around the huge workshop. The clang of metal and men working was a music I could listen to all day. It drowned out the music coming from the large, mounted speakers scattered around the room.

Back in my seat, I picked up the phone. "You still there?"

"Where the fuck else would I be?" Razor grumbled.

"It's half done. The left side of the tank is sick. The boy's got real talent. You're gonna shit yourself when you see it."

"I'll come and get it," he said excitedly. "When's Toad goin' back to the doc?"

"This afternoon. We should have a better idea about what's happening by tomorrow. You'll be coming to church, right?"

"Yeah, I shifted a few work things around so I can be there. Do you know what Killer is goin' to be discussin'?"

Linc, the club president, otherwise known as Killer, shared everything with me as his second. Razor, though a decent guy, was a nosy fuck and sometimes forgot himself. "You'll find out tomorrow with everyone else," I snapped back.

"All right, I'll see you in about half an hour." The phone went dead, but I didn't take offense. We were all the same.

"Sid, that old Buick is being a rat-ass bastard. You have ten minutes to come and have a look at it with me?" Ram asked from the doorway.

I glanced up. Ram had grease smeared over one side of his face, and the overalls he was wearing were more black than gray. The guy liked to work dirty. "Let me shut down the computer and get my overalls on."

73

He nodded and then was gone. I tidied away my desk. It was a habit I'd gotten into when I left it because too many times, I'd forget and leave everything just lying around. With my plan to go with Toad to the hospital, I wouldn't have time to come back into the office later.

Dressed in overalls, I went to Ram, shoving aside any thoughts of what was going to happen if Toad got the all-clear to go back to his apartment later today. He hadn't mentioned going home, and I hadn't brought it up. The week had officially ended, but neither of us had mentioned it.

I stared at the old Buick that had seen better days. It was a rust bucket that looked better suited for scraps. My brow furrowed. "Who thinks this is worth fixin'? It's a—"

"A fuckin' rust bucket," Ram finished for me. "Old Miss Withers, you know the old woman that has the house closest to the clubhouse?"

"Shit, I thought she'd gotten rid of this ten years ago."

"She should have. She wants me to fix her up and get her runnin' like she did. Her words, not mine." He looked anything but pleased.

"Did you try and talk her out of it?" He nodded. "Well then, I think she's dreamin', but we can try if she wants to waste money on it. Tell me what the problem is...besides the obvious."

He laughed and bent under the open hood to point out why he'd asked for my help.

💀 💀 💀

"Can't you just drop me off at the door?" Toad actually whined.

A glance sideways revealed a face set into a petulant scowl, one I wanted to kiss off his damn lips. He'd been whining since I'd picked him up ten minutes ago, and he was starting to grate on my nerves. He was the same most of the time, complaining when I had to do anything to help him. *Not in the shower*. I shut out the voice, not needing a reminder of how hard Toad made things for me, figuratively and literally.

"Shut the fuck up. We talked about this. I'm comin' in."

He slumped in the seat as I flipped the turn signal and pulled into the parking lot off to the side of the hospital. I was already sweating about stepping inside the place. Hospitals and I weren't friends, and I'd never really grown comfortable in places like these. All clean and funny-smelling.

Putting the truck I'd borrowed from the auto shop into park, I released my seatbelt and turned to stare at Toad, going for a different tack. "If they decide you need more surgery, I'll need to fill out the forms, so get over yourself."

His gaze continued to be directed at the windshield. "What if I do? Will Killer keep his word?"

There was real fear in his voice, and that's what stopped me from clipping him around the back of his head for being downright stupid. "How long have you been in the club?"

This time he looked at me. "Over a year."

"Have you ever known Killer to not mean somethin' he says?"

He shook his head, the worry lines around his mouth disappearing as his lips twitched. "I'm being a dick."

"You're always a dick, but we don't hold it against you." I joked back, then realized what I was doing. *Stop the fucking flirting!* I quickly got out of the truck, trying not to think about the wide smile on Toad's face.

The sound of the truck door slamming got me moving in the direction of the building's front entrance. Toad's booted feet hit the ground in time with mine as we walked silently into the hospital. We stopped as we entered the reception area, and I glanced at him. "You know where we're supposed to be goin'?"

"There's a map thing on the back of the letter," he rooted in his back pocket of his low-slung jeans with his left hand. He tugged out the crumpled bit of paper and gave it to me.

I read it, then looked at the signs on the beige wall. "That way." I nodded to the right.

The hallways were busy with folks in normal clothes and in different color scrubs. They all had one thing in common, they gave us a wide birth. I kept my face in a neutral mask, uncaring if folks stared. I was used to it. If it wasn't my bald tattooed head and size that made folks wary, it was the leather jacket that identified me as part of Dark Angels. Today it wasn't the leather. It was too damn hot, so I'd left it off, as had Toad. Although, he'd put on the damn hoodie for some unknown reason. As we walked down several hallways, I couldn't fail to notice how many times his head twisted from side to side. He looked like he had a problem with his neck.

"What ya doin'?"

He tripped over his feet as he glanced at me, and without thinking, I reached out to steady him. He was so close I could scent the lemon shower gel I'd used that morning to wash him. Images that had no business in my head right then left me with the urge to readjust myself.

"Thanks," he muttered, his face a dark red as his eyes searched the hallway for god knows what.

"You're actin' weird. What the fuck is it?" My fingers tightened a fraction on his arm.

"Here's not the place to talk," was his quick reply, which didn't leave me any wiser.

I let him go when he tugged his arm. "When we get back to my place, you'll be explain' yourself." I stomped off down the hallway as folks scattered like ants.

Ten minutes later, I swallowed hard at the smell coming from Toad's now-exposed hand. It filled the small room where we were waiting. The skin was wrinkled and several shades paler than his other hand. There were bits of skin that were loose where I remembered the blisters had been.

A different doctor than we'd seen before, a woman, Dr. Shore, didn't seem to notice the scent in the room as she took hold of Toad's hand to examine it. Toad pulled several faces as she pressed on some of the areas that were raw-looking.

"I'm happy with the healing. Doing the surgical scrub to remove the paint seems to have helped with skin regeneration. In my opinion, you won't need a plastic surgeon to look at this. You'll need to keep it dry and clean. I have some ointment you'll need to apply that will help stop any infection." She glanced from Toad to me then back. "Will you need to come back to the clinic to get this rebandaged every day, or do you have someone that can do it for you?"

"I can do it if you show me what I need to do," I offered before I could stop myself.

Toad's mouth opened, so I gave him a hard stare, and it shut a second later while he slumped in the chair.

"I'll have the nurse come in with everything you'll need. She'll clean your hand and dress it today so you can see what is needed." She got up and gave us both a polite smile and was gone just as quick as she arrived.

"How you gonna bandage my hand when I'm at my apartment?"

There was something about the way he spoke that suggested the question held some other meaning, yet I wasn't sure what it was.

"It's simple. You'll stay at mine."

Was it that simple?

Chapter 8

The happy feeling I got when I heard the doc say my hand didn't need any more surgery was added to when Sid offered to do the bandage changes. I was a sadistic bastard. I had to be wanting to stay with him. We had this weird kind of avoidance dance going on, and I wasn't sure this morning when he'd gone to work whether he realized I'd be heading home after the appointment. Now that wasn't happening, but there'd been no mention of how long I'd need to have my hand bandaged for. Was it wrong that I hoped it was for a very, very long time?

I swallowed the sigh when the guilt followed at the thought of my neglected work while I wasn't able to use my hand. Linc had been good to me by paying my wages. Many wouldn't have been so thoughtful; it was what I liked about being part of Dark Angels. The code of brotherhood was real. When you went from prospect to patched brother, it was like finding a new family.

And okay, there had been some of the guys I'd been wary of, and it would seem with good cause. Ned, Doddie, Stevie, and Ricky had turned their backs on the code all in the name of…fuck knows, nothing warranted turning traitor that I could see! They'd manage to corrupt some of the other members, forcing Linc's hand. He'd banded together with another club, Chosen Few, and together they'd cleaned house. There were now less than twenty-five members, and I'd gotten the feeling tomorrow there was going to be some discussion about that and what came next at the club.

A nurse bustled into the room and pulled me from my thoughts. Sid said nothing as the busty, dark-haired nurse flashed a dimpled smile at us both, but her gaze was focused on Sid. "I'm Daphne. Dr. Shore has asked me to teach you how to do a bandage change."

"Yep," Sid answered, sounding none too pleased at the prospect.

The pretty nurse upped the wattage of her smile, and I shifted on the plastic seat a little closer to Sid. The urge to put my hand on him to show my claim was fast becoming hard to resist when the woman's perfume became impossible to ignore with how close she got to us...to Sid.

I shoved my stinky hand at her. "It needs to be cleaned first."

Her nose wrinkled, but she stepped back and went over to the shelf tucked into the corner of the room. After a few seconds, she said, "I'll need to get a bowl. I'll be back in a sec."

She left the room, allowing me to breathe a little easier. Sid glanced at me, his lips a thin line, but he said nothing when the woman returned with a large metal bowl.

Hand cleaned and redressed, Sid carried the large bag of bandages and ointments that were needed for the next month that he'd gone to get from the pharmacy. I had an appointment card tucked into my back pocket for a follow-up in a month.

The bandage on my hand was much thinner than the last and gave me a little more movement. And though it throbbed from all the messing the nurse had done to it, I felt better. The only worry was getting back to the truck without making it obvious that I was apprehensive about being seen. So far, I hadn't seen anything, no sign of my family's goon squad. They'd be easy to spot in a small town like Belton.

"You're doin' that fucking head bob thing again. Seriously, are you gonna tell me what the fuck this is about?" Sid took hold of my arm and tugged me close to his body in a protective move as he steered me to the truck.

The fluttering under my breastbone left me breathless by the time we were back inside the cab of the truck. I buckled up as he did the same. The tension mounted as I tried to work out what little I could get away with and not go into the crappiness that had been my life for too many years to count.

As he drove us back to his apartment, his expression showed a determination I'd seen many times. The serpent on the side of his head seemed to stare at me as if transfixing me. Out of the truck and in his apartment, I was no further in figuring out what to tell the man who was stomping to his kitchen table to dump the bag of bandages.

When he swung around, he tilted his head to the side as he scratched at his chin. "How are we gonna do this? The easy or the hard way?"

A lump formed in my throat at what he could possibly mean by the hard way. He wasn't a man that anyone would want to cross. Would he see my past as a betrayal?

I walked to the window overlooking the parking lot in front of the auto shop, watching the cars come and go along with several bikes. "When I got out, escaped from the mental institution my family threw me in, I swore I was never goin' back. That was five years ago." I didn't look back to see how Sid took that bit of information. "My family is influential, big rollers with eyes and ears everywhere. I have no clue if they're lookin' for me or not, but I don't like to take chances. Going to the hospital is one of them."

I braced at the sound of Sid's booted feet walking across the room until they stopped behind me. The heat and scent of his body surrounded me, tempting me to lean back, to take what he had said all along he didn't want to give me. My heart ached with the need to let go and let someone else hold the burden of my past, if only for a second. But I remained still.

"Why a mental institution?"

There was nothing in the question that gave me a clue to his feelings. "I'm gay. You clearly have to be crazy to believe that about yourself?" I scoffed, sounding bitter.

The press of Sid's large body against my back was all it took for me to break. The years of yearning to be accepted were there, waiting to suck me into the dark hole of my past. His arms wrapped around my chest, and he held me tight as a sob tore from me, then another. My eyes blurred as he took my weight and said nothing.

The tears left me hollowed out and with a stuffy head, but it somehow made the ache a little less, and for the first time in years, I didn't feel so desperately alone. It was wrong to think Sid would offer more, but my heart wasn't in the mood to listen to my head. I sighed and twisted my head to look back at the man who continued to keep my body flush against his. "Thanks."

"Is your family dangerous?"

My Adam's apple bobbed twice as I forced myself to answer past my dry mouth. "They are. They are the worst kind of dangerous because they can get anyone to believe their rhetoric."

His arms tightened, and a fierce light lit his eyes. "They haven't met the Dark Angels *yet*." His voice held a dark promise of retribution I wasn't sure I was happy about.

"Maybe so, but they have a high reach that can get folks crushed with a simple nod." The fear was back, but this time it was for the man behind me. "I don't wanna seek trouble. I've lived with that most of my life and learned not to invite the devil in."

The seriousness of the situation with my family didn't seem to reach Sid, or he chose to ignore my warning. "Even the devil can find his ass bein' kicked back to Hell."

I twisted around to face the man who was threatening to take on something he didn't have any understanding of. I cupped his bristly cheeks and met his gaze, begging, "Please, I don't want to worry about you."

His brows rose as deep lines appeared around his mouth. "Why would you worry about me?"

I laid a soft kiss against his lips. "'Cause, you big fuckin' fool, I have feelings for you." I shut my eyes to block out his reaction, not needing or wanting to see the rejection.

"Fuck, shittin' hell, why do you do this to me?"

His voice was raw and full of...I wasn't sure, but it had me opening my eyes. His were dark pools of need. A need I understood because it was what I felt every time my gaze landed on this man. He lit up my insides like fucking Fourth of July fireworks, and it had only grown more intense since I'd spent more time with him. I wasn't sure I would survive what was happening between us, but I couldn't seem to stop myself.

He stepped back, and I let him go, needing him to come to me willingly, not because of some shit I'd shared with him. I didn't want his pity. No, I wanted...*more*.

"I gotta go back to work." The deep rasp of his voice caused tiny shivers to run over my body and lodge in an all too familiar place.

I nodded, not sure right then if I could speak.

Silently he left the apartment, not looking back. I slumped against the window frame and stared outside, my thoughts in turmoil.

Would Sid do something stupid like try to reach out to my family? The very idea made me sick to my stomach. In all my experience, I'd never seen anyone come up against my family and win. *You escaped!*

Yeah, by slipping out a window and nearly falling to my death. Is that really escaping? I'd never stood up to them, told them to go fuck themselves, had I? I'd skulked away in the middle of the night.

I groaned, stepping away from the window, shutting down my thoughts, knowing they would lead me nowhere but to the bottom of a bottle. Pity parties were in the past since I'd followed Sid to Belton. I'd had a purpose, a job, and a new family. More than I'd had in the first twenty-plus years of my life.

Then don't fuck it up with pinning your hopes on a man that will never give you what you want!

Chapter 9

The clubhouse was nearly full when I walked in with Toad. I'd struggled with his bandage change. It was far trickier than the nurse had made it out to be with all the different things I had to remember. It had resulted in Toad, the fucker, biting his lip as he attempted to keep still while silently laughing at me. He was lucky I hadn't punched his lights out.

My jaw ached as I took my seat next to Linc. It was only then that I noticed Mason sitting on the other side of him. *Shit*!

Why hadn't Linc mentioned Mason was coming?

I eyed the men and women in the room. There were a lot of concerned looks being fired in Linc's direction, and I got it. Never in all the club's history was I aware that a president had brought an uninitiated member into this place. It was as scared as a fucking church. My gut clenched at the possible reasons why Linc hadn't mentioned to me this was happening. Didn't he trust me?

His steely gaze landed on me as if he had read my mind. "I'll explain later," was all he said as he looked back when Matt, aka Rebel, shut the doors behind him and took a seat at the back of the room.

Silence fell, and I waited to see how this was going to go down. We'd discussed removing the option of having female prospects after the incident with Nola and had agreed to put it to a vote. The setup for Dark Angels was different from many other clubs. We'd had an inner circle of seven members who'd always made the decisions for the club. Linc's granddaddy, who'd set up Dark Angels, had left the president with the deciding vote if there was a lack of agreement.

That had worked until four of the inner circle had chosen to set up Linc by trying to remove him as president on a fake rape charge. It left the club split into sides. Some brothers had made the decision to fight against us. They'd been deposited in several hospital beds, though it didn't take away the bitter taste of betrayal. Those who'd pledged their allegiance had made a mockery of the way things had been done. Now Linc had brought Mason into church. Was that good or bad?

I had no time to consider it as Linc started talking.

"First off, Toad, it's good to hear that your hand is on the mend, and you won't need any more surgery." Linc offered a tight smile to Toad before running his hand through his hair. As Linc's gaze swept the room, he took that hand and laid it on top of Mason's.

Okay then, that was how it was going to be. A knot of anxiety formed dead center in my chest.

"There are several things I wanna talk about tonight, and *after* I've finished, I'll answer questions. I know you've all met Mason Davenport." Once more, his gaze swept the room. I wasn't sure what he was looking for as everyone remained quiet. "I've never talked about my sexual preferences. I didn't like the idea that it could be used against me. But that didn't work out so well for me." The chuckle was anything but humorous as he glanced at Mason, who remained looking relaxed sitting next to Linc.

"I'm gay. I'm not ashamed of that, and I never have been. Mason is my partner, and he'll be moving in with River and me." That got several collective gasps, and one or two members shifted on their seats. If Linc noticed, he never let on. "I'm not one for getting into anyone's business. I couldn't give two fucks who you're interested in."

"What he's trying to say is that your sexual preferences make no difference to him or Dark Angels," Mason said, getting everyone in the room to look at him, including a very frustrated-looking Linc.

"I told you I'd deal with it," he growled.

Mason shrugged, remaining in a relaxed posture.

Linc glanced back at the others. "What he said. There will be no judgment between brothers. If you don't like that, then there's the door." Linc nodded toward the entrance to the room, his gaze narrowing as it moved to meet every member one by one.

There was the sound of a curse before Ren, aka Beanpole, stood without saying anything, giving Linc a disgusted glare before he turned, walking to the door.

"Leave your jacket in the clubhouse," I called after him.

Linc laid a hand on my arm, pulling my attention to how tense I was. Adrenaline pumped through me as if I were preparing to fight.

"It's fine," Linc muttered low enough for only me to hear.

One look at his masked features, and I sat back, my foot tapping on the floor.

"Anyone else want to leave?" Linc's impenetrable stare moved over those in front of us.

Every member, in turn, shook their heads, allowing a little of the tension to release from my shoulders.

"Now that's out of the way, I've also asked Mason here tonight for another reason. In the past, some of you have used the weasel, Winters, as your lawyer. Because he was involved with Nola Fink and the traitors who set me up on false rape charges, he's fuckin' off-limits. If you're in need of a lawyer, you'll come to Mason, and he'll figure out who is the best to deal with your issues. Winters gets no more business from this club, is that understood?" The edge of aggression to his Linc's voice could have cut through metal.

Once more, there were nods of agreement. After that, Mason left, and Linc continued to lay out the changes. "There is no longer an inner circle. I talked to Sid about creating another, but I've decided against that. You will all be involved in any future decisions about this club. As president, I'll listen and go with the majority vote. There is a list of new prospects, and on it are several women." Linc's gave traveled to the three out of four female members present tonight since Nutty was, I assumed, with River. "Your first vote is to decide if women are to be accepted as prospects."

Melinda, aka Ballbreaker, one of the longest affiliated members of the club, gave Linc a smile of approval.

"I want a show of hands for the current practice to carry on."

No one rose their hand.

"It's unanimous no more females as prospects."

After that, there were several more votes on general business around the club, the bar, and then it got to anyone who had an issue with a club member that needed resolving. All in all, the meeting went better than I expected.

Two hours later, I sat next to Linc at the bar, sipping a beer. "Why didn't you say Mason was coming tonight?"

His brows rose at the bite of anger I hadn't concealed. "'Cause I didn't know he was comin' until he told me when we were leavin' the house." Dark-red rode over his cheekbones as he glanced down at the beer he held. "The fucker is a manipulative bastard."

Laughter that I couldn't swallow at how put out he sounded roared out of me. Several heads turned in our direction, but I didn't pay them any attention as I wiped at my eyes, finding it difficult to control my amusement. "You're cock-whipped."

A solid punch was aimed at my arm. I gasped from the pain that shot through to my elbow as it hit the edge of the bar. "Motherfucker." I dropped my beer on the bar, the glass ringing against the wood, before rubbing at my throbbing elbow.

Toad appeared in my line of sight, his face showing a wealth of concern he didn't try to mask. I kept my attention on Linc, hoping he wouldn't notice Toad. After his announcement about being gay and how others in the club should be accepting, I had a feeling Toad might take that as a sign to reveal what had been going on between us.

My heart sped up as excitement I refused to admit to aloud ran through me.

Years of verbal abuse had left internal scars I didn't like to pick at. It was easier to avoid internal shit in my experience. Yet Toad left me unsure about whether that was good or bad. I wasn't sure I was ready for what that meant to him, to me, if I picked at the scars. His confession earlier about his family left too many unanswered questions that could result in him wanting my story.

Putting that worry back in the box, I shoved it to the back of my mind, focusing on what information Toad had given me when he'd completed the work application form. A thought niggled. Was the name he'd given real?

The question left me searching him out as Matt came to talk to Linc about some work he'd asked Matt to do for Mina, the woman who was River's babysitter.

Glancing back to Toad, he sat alone nursing his beer next to the pool table, watching Melinda and Davey play pool. As I sat and watched him, it struck how he tended to sit on the outskirts of any group, not quite joining in. Just there, observing others with those sorrowful eyes. Why hadn't I noticed that before?

Maybe because you've been running from the attraction between you? The snarky voice was ignored as I picked back up my beer to take a deep swallow to wet my mouth.

"—ride out."

There was a nudge to my arm, and I returned my attention to the two men looking at me expectantly. "What?" I growled in discomfort, hoping like hell I'd kept the thoughts off my face.

"The plan for the next ride out. Have you sorted where we're going?" Matt asked as his gaze moved from me to Toad and back. His dark brows rode up his forehead, speculation lighting up his eyes.

"I promised Rattlesnake we'd head back up to Little Rock to party with him and his brothers. Fuck, I should have mentioned that in church." The new rules about getting a collective vote of agreement, would that have included a ride out?

Linc slammed his hand on the bar, drawing every eye in the room to him. "Next ride out, is everyone happy to go back to Little Rock?"

"Hell yeah."

"Right on."

"As long as the bar is stocked."

It went on like that as the members all spoke over each over until Linc shouted, "One at a fuckin time."

There was laughter and some ribbing before it was agreed that I'd sort a ride out with Rattlesnake to book the cabin we'd used last time.

As the evening wore on, I found my gaze moving back time and time again to Toad. "Linc, you got a half an hour tomorrow to have a private chat?" I wasn't aware I was going to ask until the words came out of my mouth.

"Off the top of my head, I think the schedule for the day is full," his brows rose, "but that's never stopped you before."

"It's private."

"We can go out the back to the apartment now if it's important?"

I weighed that option but decided against it. I needed to tread carefully with Toad, his fear was real, and I wasn't sure how he'd react to me sharing with Linc. Up to now, he'd kept his past hidden from his brothers, it seemed for good reasons. It wasn't something the club members were ever forced to do, share their lives, not unless it affected the club. Did this have the potential to impact the club? It would if Toad's family came looking for him.

"Tomorrow. I need to talk to...someone first. I'll ring Nutty in the morning to see if you can squeeze me in."

The inscrutable expression he gave me was followed by a curt nod. He changed the subject onto my next tattoo, and I breathed easier. Then I glanced once more at Toad.

Tomorrow. I'd talk to him tomorrow.

Chapter 10

TOAD

The warmth of the bed didn't encourage me to want to move because I'd slept for shit. Sid had acted stranger than normal last night. He'd driven us back to his apartment, and there hadn't been any conversation due to the hard mask and thin-lipped expression on his face that was about as inviting as going swimming in shark-infested waters. I'd left him to it and gone to bed. Instead of sleeping, I'd stewed over what had caused it for hours. The only thing I could come up with was maybe it was Mason being invited into church. Sid hadn't hidden his surprise, or not well, when he'd eyed the other man sitting next to Linc. Was that the issue? Or was it something to do with me? With the number of times Sid had looked in my direction, I wasn't wholly convinced it wasn't me that had put the worry lines around his mouth. Neither were the fireflies lighting up my innards since Linc had made it clear to everyone that being gay in Dark Angels was only to be met with acceptance. Would that make a difference to Sid? Was that what had put up the 'keep away' sign on his face?

My heart thudded against my ribs at the sound of heavy footfalls in the hallway right before Sid shouted outside the bedroom door, "You getting up, or are you gonna lay in bed all day? Some of us have jobs to do."

Shower time. It was both the worst and the best part of my day. When Sid had gone to the pharmacy in the hospital to get my bandages and ointment, I'd asked the nurse about showering and getting my hand wet. She'd said I could take off the bandages to shower. As long as I didn't leave my hand in the water for too long, then I'd be fine. Had I told Sid that? *Nope.* Was it bad of me? *Hell, yeah.* But since I was the only one paying for it with a hard-on that hadn't quit for days, I couldn't see the harm. I rolled my eyes heavenward at how lame I was being.

The door opened, making me realize I hadn't bothered to answer Sid. He scowled when he saw I was awake and very much alert as my cock tented the covers. I wasn't going to be embarrassed by how my body reacted to him. I wasn't. With heat flooding up my chest and neck, I shoved the covers off my naked body and rolled off the bed.

Naked and aroused, I stood and tortured myself some more with the weight of Sid's heavy-lidded gaze roaming over my body.

His hands clenched at his sides as he stalked to the bathroom doorway. "I haven't got all day," he ground out.

By the time I'd swallowed the chuckle and followed him into the bathroom, he'd switched on the shower. The T-shirt came of next while I struggled to swallow. His hands never ventured to the shorts he wore. As usual, he left them in place though they did little to conceal his heavy arousal that pushed at the soft fabric. I really wanted to tug the fuckers right off his body. To date, I'd resisted the temptation, but it was a battle I had with myself every damn day.

"Get in and stop lookin' at me like that."

He sounded mean and bad tempted, that only made me ache for him more, sick bastard that I was. The one time we'd had sex, it had been hard and rough, but I'd been the one doing the fucking. I'd sensed that Sid's preference might lean toward being a power bottom, and I'd been right. Although he didn't like to acknowledge what he craved verbally, his actions had more than spoken for him, and that was fine with me. I was versatile and would take him any way he wanted.

I gave him a slow sexy smile as I stroked my uninjured hand over my cock. "How exactly am I lookin' at you?"

The impatient snarl was followed by him knocking my hand away from my cock. I shook my head and stepped into him. "You don't get to decide if I touch myself." I dropped my voice. "You know that."

I took hold of my cock once more and stroked from base to tip, making a show of it as his eyes traveled down my body and a hungry look appeared. "You want to taste, want to suck me hard and deep in your throat till you choke?" I whispered seductively.

His large, tattooed chest shuddered as his fingers flexed then curled into tight balls at his side.

"Get on your knees," I growled low and mean.

There was a moment of hesitation, and I cursed myself for pushing, then he sank down, cutting off the air to my chest at this powerful man getting on his knees for me. I lifted my cock in reward, offering it to him. This time there was no hesitation as his tongue came out and swirled over the slick head, gathering up the beads of precum before his tongue disappeared into his mouth. He groaned as he swallowed, then he came forward, his lips parting to suck the mushroom head of my cock into the warmth of his wet mouth. The visual combined with the sensations left my legs shaking in mere seconds, yet he didn't seem to notice as his eyelids fluttered down.

His tongue slid around the head to the underside to tease the bundle of nerves there. Warm tingles spread over my body. Several times his tongue slipped and slithered around the head until he dipped his tongue into my slit. The shaking in my legs increased with his moans vibrating over my hard flesh. My nipples pebbled as the room grew steamy and thick with sexual tension.

He worshiped the head of my cock for long minutes until I was on the brink and breathless with the need to thrust deep in his throat. I squeezed the base of my cock, willing my orgasm back, unsure if he'd want more than what we were doing. "I wanna fuck you," I rasped low and deep, keeping my gaze on him.

Eyes wild with need opened as a whine escaped before he drew back to release my cock. There was so much uncertainty clouding the need that I wanted to wrap my arms around him. The seconds stretched; the only sound in the room was the water hitting the titled floor behind me.

"I don't have time...*now*." His eyelashes dipped to shield his thoughts as his mouth claimed my dick. His hand came up, and he gently removed my hand from the base of my cock. Quickly following this, his mouth slid down my shaft until his nose touched my skin. Deep-throating was something that left me struggling to keep control. Especially when Sid placed his large hands on my hips to hold me in place, then mouth-fucked me hard and fast.

Slurping wet noises followed as my eyes drifted closed, feeling too heavy to stay open with the assault on my senses. Multiple feelings chased each other as his fingers kneaded at my flesh hard enough to leave marks. The head of my cock hit the back of his throat repeatedly as he swallowed and clasped the head in a velvety, wet kiss.

It didn't take long before I was groaning. I threw back my head as my cock throbbed painfully, then gave Sid everything he was demanding with his greedy mouth. Pulse after pulse slid down his throat as he eased off and sucked at the softening, sensitive flesh. His tongue lapped twice over my slit to make sure he missed none of my cum before he released me fully.

Replete, lethargy stole my ability to keep upright, collapsing forward, my good hand going to Sid's shoulder as I rested my forehead on top of his bald head. "Fucker," I groaned through my dry lips.

His hands held me steady until I recovered enough to stand without fear of falling over. One look at him left me with a sinking feeling. Wariness was etched into his tight features as he wordlessly helped me into the shower, ever mindful of my hand, and went through the routine of washing me. The gentle care he took of me said more than any words that he cared for me. I knew he did. He was just too fucking stubborn to admit it.

The evidence of his arousal became more apparent as the water hit his shorts and plastered them to his skin. The temptation to reach out was tempered by the continued wariness he didn't hide. Out of the shower, he grabbed a towel and helped to dry me, even when he really didn't need to.

The fluttering under my ribcage that persisted whenever he acted this way toward me got a real workout by the time he'd left the bedroom. Silently he closed the door behind him as I sat on the edge of the bed. Had that broken his rule of no repeats? He hadn't sucked my cock before, so essentially, I'd say it hadn't. Would he see it like that?

There was no real answer when Sid was more closed off than a highway under construction. That begged the question of whether I should speak to someone that knew him well enough to answer some of the questions about the enigmatic guy?

You don't like people poking into your life.

My shoulders sagged as I stared at the door. I didn't, but that didn't mean it wasn't going to happen now I'd opened up to Sid. Was he going to want me to talk to the brothers about my past? I attempted to shove the sense of dread that accompanied that question to the back of my mind. But it wouldn't take the hint to fuck off.

Where did that leave me then?

With choices you might not like!

Chapter 11

SID

Sun glinted off my sunglasses as I pulled into the open garage. The heat in the concrete box left me wishing I'd left off my leather jacket. Motorcycle parked in Linc's garage, I removed my jacket and open-faced helmet, leaving them on my hog.

There was no breeze, only a wall of heat as I exited the garage and walked up to the house where Linc worked and lived. The place was nothing like I'd imagined when he'd first talked about moving his business and buying someplace. He'd wanted to be closer to River if she needed him, and this had been his solution, a house in suburbia.

When he'd brought me here to show me the three-story house in the middle of a suburban neighborhood, I'd thought he'd lost his mind. I was convinced the folks on this street would have a lot to say about the president of a biker club living on their doorstep. I'd been surprised that, though there had been some grumblings, Mina, one of the neighbors, led the charge in showing everyone that Linc and River were good people. It had worked to a degree, and for the most part, Linc had been left alone, though I secretly thought that had a lot more to do with his affiliation with Dark Angels.

I walked up the drive to the steps leading to the front porch. The tattoo shop was housed on the ground floor, so I stepped through the door without knocking. Nutty glanced up from whatever she was looking at on the wooden counter she worked behind. The phone, as always, was tucked to her ear, her dark hair an array of spikes making her look a little like a porcupine. Not that I'd ever mention that to her, not if I wanted to keep my balls where they were.

She rolled her amused eyes at me and mouthed, "Go on up."

I'd called ahead to find out when Linc had five minutes to talk, so I nodded and left her to the phone call. I glanced into the waiting area and nodded to a couple of guys I recognized that used the auto shop.

There were a few speculative looks from a group of girls sitting in the corner. I kept moving to the staircase in front of me. The wooden stairs creaked as I went up to the second floor where both Linc and Kyle, one of the other tattoo artists, worked. I gave a brief knock on Linc's door before sticking my head in. He was standing at the large counter that ran down one side of the room where all his gear was stored. As usual, he didn't acknowledge me as he finished cleaning his tattoo gun.

Aware that he'd wait me out before speaking, I roamed to the window. This morning's entertainment was still at the forefront of my mind. Toad was irresistible, his moves practiced, and he seemed to know exactly what buttons to press to get me to do what he wanted. Is that so? Or is that you just want him more than anyone you've ever encountered? Whatever it was, the ache in my chest to deny him what he wanted wasn't something I liked or wanted.

"You're broodin'."

"Maybe," I answered, not looking back at the man moving around behind me.

"What's up?" Leather creaked as Linc sighed.

"It's not the club," I assured him before I turned around. "It's Toad."

Lines appeared around his mouth. "The doc said his hand was healing. Last night you never brought up that there were any issues, so what is it?"

I rubbed a hand over my bald head, registering that it needed a shave before I met Linc's unfathomable gaze. "I didn't mention anything last night because it's kinda...personal."

His brows shot up, and the seat creaked once more, but he waited for me to continue. Linc had the whole silent act down to pat, and I started to sweat even with the knowledge I'd asked to talk to him. "Toad was actin' weird when we went to the hospital."

"So he doesn't like the place, how many of us do?" Impatience was stamped over Linc's face as he eyed the clock and moved his hand to encourage me to get to the point.

"I haven't asked him if it's okay to talk about this, so bear with me," I gritted out through clenched teeth before I could rein back my temper. "Quick rundown. When he hurt his hand, he was insistent he didn't need the hospital. It was more than your 'I hate hospitals.' I couldn't work it out. Then when we went for the appointment, he was actin' like I'd stuck fire ants down his pants, jumpin' all over the place. When I got him back to the apartment, he confessed his family members are big hitters. That they'd locked him in a mental institution because he's gay."

That got Linc off the chair. "For real? His family locked him away for being gay?"

The charged anger in the room could have been Linc's or mine. What I'd said hit just as hard as it had the first time I'd heard Toad explain it. "That's what he's tellin' me, and I believe him. He's got no reason to lie, and he wasn't happy about me pumpin' him for information either."

"How long has it been since he's had any contact with his family? And do you think that shit is gonna follow him here?"

I shrugged, unable to really answer the second part, except my gut reaction was yes. "Five years, he's not sure they're still lookin' for him. The way he was, I'd suggest he knows deep down that they're still searchin' for him. My gut thinks that too."

"Fuck. This should have been discussed with the other members. We can't protect him if we aren't aware of his fucking shit."

The second he uttered those words, the tension that had been with me since Toad had told me a little of his back story, released. The protection of Dark Angels was what I wanted, what I needed to keep Toad safe. It was humbling to realize his safety was all I was bothered about, but that wasn't what I wanted to dwell on then. "As I said, I haven't told him I was gonna talk to you about it, and he ain't gonna be happy," I muttered, feeling like crap from betraying him.

Linc gave me a hard stare. "Fuck's sake, you keep coming with the hits." He ran his hands through his long hair. "Go and fuckin' talk to him, then bring him to the club Friday. I'll call an emergency meetin'. I'll ask Mason to come too. He might be able to offer some advice."

Even the fact he was offering Mason's help showed how serious Linc was taking the threat. His trust toward the other man showed how much his feelings for Mason had grown. Envy curled in the pit of my stomach at how open and honest Linc was about his relationship.

When I'd called Mason at the time Linc had zoned out on us after the beatdown with the traitors, there'd been no way to anticipate what had happened. The declaration of love from Mason toward Linc had been shocking to hear. What had been more shocking was how much I'd wanted to be the one on the receiving end of such devotion. Not from Mason...

It was impossible to finish the thought when I'd done what I always do when I hid from the reality of my life. I'd gone to Austin to find a fuck buddy to dispel any stupid thoughts of wanting more. How did that work out for you?

My guts clenched right along with my ass at the memory of Toad owning me, of reading me too fucking well to give me the things I only thought about alone and in the dark.

A punch to my arm drew my gaze to Linc. "What?"

He shook his head. "Whatever you're daydreaming about has no place in this fuckin' conversation." His gaze dipped, and heat spread over my head when the throbbing going on in my jeans became more than a little noticeable.

Shit!

"Sorry," I mumbled, avoiding looking him in the eye.

"Whatever, man. Go and talk to Toad. We need to know what the threat is regardless of how long it's been since he's seen his family."

There was a knock at the door before Nutty appeared with a huge dude behind her. "Your next appointment is here." She shifted sideways, and I got a good look at the guy.

He was built like a tank. The T-shirt he wore was plastered to a wall of muscles. His huge arms were covered in tattoos. His gaze was as assessing as mine as it swept over me before he glanced in Linc's direction. "Linc." He tipped his head.

"Benny, come in." Linc stared pointedly at me. "Sort it out and call me later."

With that, I left not feeling confident I'd done the right thing, but it was too late now.

Would Toad see I'd done this to protect him? Or see it as me interfering? It was a toss-up.

Back on my hog, I rode back to the auto shop. Ten minutes later, I parked out front and sat staring at the display window. Three motorcycles were gleaming in the window. They were swapped out every two days. Customers who received a custom paint job were offered the chance to have them displayed in the window. Ninety percent of them agreed, and it was a great advertisement for Toad's skills. The white backdrop left you nothing to look at but the artwork. And it was art. Once more, I recalled I'd forgotten to ask him what he'd designed for my bike.

I swung my leg off the bike and glanced up at my apartment windows. The man stood, his eyes revealing nothing as he stared at me. Shoving away the long list of jobs I had planned for the afternoon, I headed around the back of the building. I rolled my shoulders, taking several deep breaths of the warm air: grease and oil-filled my nose as I walked past the entrance to the workshop.

"You got a minute?" Ram called out.

"Later," I shouted back, not looking in his direction. If I got collared now, there was no guarantee I hadn't decide to do the avoiding thing.

The door unlocked, I headed upstairs. I hesitated as my fingers trembled. "Get over yourself," I muttered as I opened the door.

Toad was facing me as if he'd known I was coming. "You spoke to Killer, didn't you?"

He sounded resigned more than pissed, so I jumped right in. "I did. The protection of our brothers is key. You know this. We look out for our own."

A defiant light appeared in his eyes. "Is that all this is? One brother protectin' another?"

The denial was there on the tip of my tongue, yet I held it back. "Both, but you can't read any more into it. I've told you, this," my hand moved between us, "ain't happening."

"I call bullshit. It's already happening. You need to fucking stop hiding behind your shit and own your fuckin' feelings. You're gonna pull some crap and tell me I need to fuckin' share my past, yet you ain't gonna apply that to yourself." His good hand clenched and unclenched at his side before he swung around and stomped to the kitchen.

There was no point denying what he so aptly summarized. He was right. I was going to tell him he needed to share. Sharing why I had so many insecurities about my sexuality was a delve into a barrel of dead fish that I'd avoided that my whole adult life. Doing it now filled me with nothing but dread. The band constraining my chest said I was about to do something I loathed.

Toad got a beer from the fridge and cracked the top on the counter to get rid of the lid. Beer frothed out of the bottle before he could take a mouthful. It ran down his chin as he stuck the head of the bottle between his lips.

Walking to the window where Toad had just been moments ago, I placed my hands on the ledge in front of me, hoping it would stop them from revealing how I was shaking as I kicked hard at the wall my past was hidden behind. "I grew up in Belton's downtown area. It was a dump and a place no one would choose to willingly live in. I don't know who my ma was. The asshole that raised me said she ran off after taking one look at my ugly face." I laughed grimly as the old hurt wanted to get me in a chokehold.

An ache developed behind my eyes as I stared out the window, seeing only the ugly bastard who'd claimed to be my family gazing back at me. "There was only him and me. He hated me, yet he couldn't seem to find it in him to get rid of me. I've long since given up trying to figure it out. Maybe it was 'cause I was an easy punchin' bag." I shut my eyes on the years of pain, of abuse, that I'd endured. "He was a racist as well as a homophobic asshole. Anyone different from him was treated with hate and distrust."

I jerked as arms wrapped around my chest from behind. I glanced sideways into troubled eyes. The pain was unexpected, but the lack of pity allowed me to carry on. "I'm not sure if he sensed I was different before I even figured it out myself. The beatings got so bad that social services came to the house. It was then that Linc's granddaddy came callin'.

"I don't know how he persuaded the old man to let me move into the clubhouse. I don't really care. I went willingly, and I never looked back. The old fucker died a few years later, and that was that." Even as it passed my lips, I knew it hadn't been. The years of listening to his crap had left a mark inside me, one I'd chosen to ignore until now.

Toad pressed his lips against mine in a soft kiss, one I would swear I didn't need, but the way my mouth clung to his said something different.

"Families, who fucking needs them," he mouthed softly against my lips before he eased back, giving me a little breathing room. "What do you want me to do?"

He wore a resigned expression as I stared at him, trying to control the wealth of emotions his simple offer did to me. "Talk to the brothers on Friday so we know what to be ready for if those chasin' you come callin'." It sounded so simple, yet I understood it was anything but that.

"Okay, but you gotta promise me one thing."

"What?" I asked cautiously.

"You won't go lookin' for trouble." His jaw was clenched as he went rigid, waiting for me to answer.

"I swear I won't go lookin' for trouble as long as whoever is lookin' for you stays away."

He nodded slowly. "Deal."

Chapter 12

TOAD

Whatever I'd thought was going to happen next between Sid and me, it didn't. The worry of what I was expected to share with my brothers tonight kept my head firmly occupied. The last two days had dragged while I'd written down the things I felt I could share. The list was short, too short when I considered what I'd already shared with Sid.

The man had been unapologetic for sharing my business, yet a part of me had known the second I opened up that this would be the path it would take me down. I'd been with Dark Angels for long enough to understand this was how it worked with my brothers. They'd want to protect one of their own.

"You ready to go?" Sid asked.

I spun around to face him standing in the doorway of my bedroom. His expression was broody. Dressed in tight-fitting jeans, ripped at the knees, his T-shirt was black with a serpent coiled in the center of his chest. The eyes were similar to those of the man. His bald head gleamed as if it had been polished. A sign he'd recently shaved it. The first time I'd seen him, I'd wondered if he'd been going bald and why he shaved his head. It turned out he hated the curls that grew fast and furious if he let it grow. He preferred to be bald. The tattoo on the side of his skull made a statement much like the man, one that said mess with me and suffer the consequences. Why was I so drawn to him?

The answer alluded me as I twisted and reached down for my leather jacket. "Yeah, I'm ready." If my voice lacked any real conviction, Sid ignored it as he spun and walked back into the hallway. I followed at a slower pace.

Out in the evening sun, sweat slid down my spine as I put on my jacket, followed by my helmet. Once Sid was seated on his bike, I climbed on the back and tried not to think about where my groin was now nestled.

Using my left arm, I slipped it around his waist and held on. He stiffened, then relaxed as the engine throbbed with power under us. He took off at speed, forcing me to hold on a little tighter. Riding on his bitch seat messed with my head. I was no one's bitch, but I liked how close riding like this allowed me to get to him.

I tucked into his body and went with the natural flow, leaning into the bends as Sid rode without caution. I missed riding my own motorcycle. The freedom of the open road gave me confidence that I could go anywhere, leave anytime I wanted. I'd been trapped for too many years, and my damaged hand only seemed to remind me of what it was like to not be free to do as I pleased.

The sigh was lost to the wind as Sid increased his speed as if he sensed my mood and was trying to chase it away. Minutes later, he stopped outside the club. With the hog on its stand, he waited for me to get off the back.

No longer having the wind to buffer the heat, I started to melt in my leather jacket. My sweaty skin stuck to the lining inside the jacket, causing me to struggle to remove it. In my frustration, I unwittingly smacked into Sid, who'd come up behind me silently.

"Fuck's sake, let me help," he gritted out, impatient as ever.

Yet, his hands were far gentler than his tone as he messed about for a few seconds to free my hand. Leather jacket off, I went to undo the strap on my helmet. Sid carefully knocked my hand away. He didn't meet my gaze as I stared at him, seeing a side to him that he rarely showed to others. He had a wealth of love to give if he'd only open up to the possibility.

"What's this?" Razor called from somewhere behind me.

The instant stiffening in Sid's body left me wondering for a second if he was going to pull away. My eyes widened when he didn't and continued to undo the strap under my chin.

"If you can't see, then you need fuckin' spectacles," Sid growled.

"Funny fucker," Razor mumbled before there was the sound of booted feet moving over wood.

"I'm sorry," I found myself saying.

"Drop it."

Doing as he asked, I waited until he moved back before taking off my helmet and hanging it on the handlebar.

Inside the club, I nodded to several of the guys as I walked directly to the bar. I kept my gaze away from Sid, who'd gone over to where Linc was sitting with Mason.

"Hey, Mel, a beer when you're ready."

"Give me a sec," she nodded toward Ram. "Just sortin' Ram out."

There was laughter from Razor and Kink, who were stood on the other side of Ram. Melinda rolled her eyes at the pair of them. "Dicks for brains."

Razor grabbed at his groin and bared his teeth. "Any time you wanna try out my brain, it's waitin' here for you."

"What would your old lady say about that?" Kink said, his voice full of amusement. Fin was aptly named Kink as it appeared, he was into anything and everything to do with sex.

Color flooded Razor's face as he glanced warily about the large room. "Don't go mentioning the old lady. I'm fuckin' convinced she has me bugged." He gave a mock shudder as he grabbed his bottle off the bar and drunk deep.

His old lady wasn't a member of the club, and I'd only met her once, and that had been enough. All the woman had done was nag and bitch, it seemed, about everything. I wasn't sure why Razor stayed with her.

"She needs to keep tabs on you, for sure. You keep forgetting to keep your dick zipped." Melinda shook her head as she placed my beer on the bar.

I reached into my pocket to grab my wallet. Fear spiked hard and fast as someone came up behind me and held my hand trapped against my body at a painful and awkward angle. Without thinking, I kicked my leg back, aiming for the kneecap of whoever held me. There was a loud yowl as I was immediately released. This was followed by a thump that I felt under my feet.

Sucking in a shaky breath, I turned slowly only to find everyone seemed to be focused on me. On the floor, clutching his kneecap, was one of the newer members, Nuts, AKA Deacon, who'd been a new prospect around the same time as me.

Fuck's sake!

"Sorry, man," I muttered as I crouched down and offered him my left hand to help him up. I didn't dare look in Sid's direction as he remained seated. Was he going to think I was losing my shit?

Nuts rubbed at his knee twice more, eyeing my hand warily. "It's ok. I shouldn't have been messin' with you." He didn't sound apologetic. He sounded pissed.

"Let me buy you a beer."

He nodded, ignoring my outstretched hand. Once he was up, he hobbled past me as I stood to follow him. There were several speculative looks aimed at me before the guys went back to talking shit. Beer in hand, Nuts limped off to the pool table while I leaned against the bar to sip my beer. I stood to the side, just listening to the guys talk about whatever was going on in their lives.

"Let's head to church," Linc called out loud enough for everyone to hear.

The noise in the main clubhouse increased to a deafening level as guys grabbed their drinks and took off in the direction of the large meeting room. Not in a rush to face what was coming, I finished my beer then headed to the restroom before finally going into church. Linc didn't give me a chance to take a seat at the back of the room where I liked to sit. He raised his hand and pointed to the seat right next to Sid. The beer swished in my gut as I went and took the seat, doing my best to avoid looking directly at anyone in front of me. Now that I was here, I wasn't sure I wouldn't puke.

The conversations around the room hushed when Linc raised one hand in the air. Once the room was silent, the hand dropped, and Linc glanced in my direction. "You happy for me to start?"

"As I'll ever be."

Mason shifted in his seat and gave me a sympathetic smile. Had Linc shared with him what I'd told Sid?

"Toad has some personal things he needs to share. It goes without sayin' this ain't for sharing outside of this room. Once he starts talkin' in here, it becomes club business." The authority rolled off Linc as he pointed out the obvious.

Everyone nodded at that, but all eyes were now on me. I licked at my lips and wished I'd thought to get another beer. "I'm not sure where to start," I muttered, hating that heat was creeping up my neck.

"Wherever, man," Knobby shouted, getting several laughs.

Linc growled low and mean, getting instant silence.

Seeing no way out, I inhaled a deep breath, held it, hoping to calm the anxiety working its way from my guts up into my chest. "I have what you'd call a bigoted family." I swallowed when Sid shifted a fraction closer to me. "I'm gay. For that, they locked me in a mental institution, telling everyone who'd listen I was crazy."

There were several gasps but thankfully not from the gay part. Linc's steely gaze when it met mine caused a shiver to race down my spine. His name never more apt at that moment, Killer.

Was he pissed at me, or what happened? I wasn't sure. And I couldn't get a read off him. He was closed down too tightly.

Mason laid a hand on Linc's arm. "Who is your family?"

This was the part I'd been dreading. I'd been honest with the name I'd given them. I'd just chosen to drop my surname and use my middle name in its place. "One you might have heard of." It was as if everyone was holding their breath collectively as I glanced forward. "My father is William Mark Hanna."

There were a couple of blank faces, but the majority seemed to have heard of the man that was a third-generation industrialist who invested greatly in the Republican Party, as had my granddaddy and his father before him. As the oldest son and per the stipulations of my granddaddy's will, I was supposed to inherit my fortune when I turned twenty-five. But I'd been a huge regret to my old man. As far as he was concerned, he preferred I rot in a mental hospital for the rest of my life and lose all rights to my inheritance.

Sid was the first to break the silence. "That's not the name you use."

The accusation in his voice hit home. Pain bloomed in the center of my chest at the distrust he didn't hide as I glanced at him. "I gave you my real name, Mark Wyatt. It's my first and second name. I dropped the surname when I managed to escape the hospital. There was no way I could chance giving my surname. Don't you see?" I hated the begging tone, but Sid's face had become so closed off that panic was taking hold.

"What about when you became a brother? What about then?" Sid fired back before I could continue to explain.

"Would that have been wise given everything that has happened recently, Sid?" Mason asked, the voice of reason in a room that was fast filling with tension.

Sid shifted, the scowl deepening as his lips thinned. Folks started to fidget in their seats while looks of uncertainty appeared as if they were contagious, passing from one person to the next.

Linc stood and started to pace. It was something I'd seen him do when he wanted to think something through. "I think you need to explain a little more about what the real issues are."

It wasn't a question, so I swallowed the sigh at having to delve into something I tried to avoid, talking about my family.

Chapter 13

The betrayal felt huge. It pressed against my chest, making it difficult to take a deep breath. I got that Toad needed to hide, yet, a part of me struggled to comprehend why he hadn't shared this with me. Shared something as vital as his name. He did. Mark Wyatt is his name! I closed out the voice of reason, not wanting to hear it right then as Toad started to talk.

"I was thirteen, maybe fourteen, when I started to take an interest in boys. I can't say I ever had a great relationship with the old man. He is an opinionated asshole who has one belief." His brow furrowed. "He's never wrong and his opinion is the only one that matters. I'm not sure how he got wind that I'd kissed another boy in the private school he was paying a fortune for. I was hauled out and brought home to Washington State. From there, it all went to shit. I was homeschooled, and the gay...was to be removed forcibly from me."

Bile burned my throat at the matter-of-fact way he spoke. It was almost like he was talking about someone else.

"Did your mother not intervene?" Mason asked gently.

The laugh sounded bitter and cold. "She only does as Father says. He picked her because she has the same beliefs as he does." His shoulders shrugged.

Mason's face was a mask of concern. "I think maybe we need to continue this conversation in private."

Linc stopped pacing and glanced at Mason, shaking his head. "That isn't how we do things. Everyone needs to know what the potential threat is."

Mason stood, and the silence in the room was deafening as both men faced each other. I'd seen Mason in action before after the beatdown at the cabin. The man could be as bull-headed as Linc.

"I understand y'all need to know this risk, but getting Toad to spill his guts in front of everyone, is that really what's needed? I'd suggest Toad go through what he feels are the risks and leave his painful past right where it belongs, in the past." Mason's face showed no signs of fear as Linc glared at him.

"This is club business."

"Then you shouldn't have invited me in to listen." He glanced at Toad, who looked anything but happy to be the center of attention right then. "What influences did your family use to get you locked up? Did they use their political power? Their money? How did they get you certified? Friends or blackmail?" His gaze moved back to Linc, whose face was dark and dangerous. "These are the things we need to know. It's how I'll protect you and your brothers."

Linc never got a chance to say a word as Mason swung around and headed for the exit.

"Fuck's sake!" Linc bellowed at Mason's stiff back as he disappeared out the door.

"This is going well," Toad muttered, just loud enough that I caught it.

Club members stared at Linc as he returned to his seat, then glanced at Toad. "Can you answer all those questions?" he gritted out between clenched teeth.

"I can… Do you want me to do it now?" Toad asked hesitantly, his gaze shifting nervously to the other members and back to Linc.

"We'll vote on it."

The vote turned out to be unanimous for Toad to explain his shit now. He lost a little of his color, but he started to go through each of Mason's questions one at a time. By the time he'd finished, Linc looked no less pleased, and some of the members were eyeing Toad with a lot more respect.

"How did you manage with no money?" Matt asked when Toad finally stopped speaking.

Toad shifted in the seat next to me, his gaze firmly fixed forward when he answered, "I worked the streets. Folks will pay for sex."

The seat I was on fell with a crash as I stood and stalked out of the room. The bile that had continued to burn my throat throughout Toad's conversation wasn't staying put. I burst through the restroom door, running for the sink as brown vomit spewed over the white porcelain. It burned my chest, throat, and nose as my stomach repeatedly heaved, not letting up for a second. Sweat coated my body as I shook and shivered. Vileness coated my mouth, and the scent in the room became unbearable, adding to my woes.

A vague noise behind me brought me back and aware that I'd left the door open, but right then, I didn't have the strength to do more than cling to the edge of the sink until my body emptied itself. Long minutes seemed to pass before I felt able to raise my blurry gaze to the mirror above the sink I was clinging to. Toad stood behind me, pale with apparent fear shining bright in his eyes.

Time stood still as I wiped a hand over my mouth while we stared at each other silently. The question was there for me to see. Had what he'd told me made a difference to what—had been happening between us—I'd chosen to pretend wasn't real? All it did was make me sick to my stomach at the thoughts of him having to...

Yeah, there was no way I could think about that and not want to heave.

"I'm sorry."

"For what?" I snapped, then sighed. I shut my eyes to close out his hurt expression. "Give me a minute."

There was a sound, and when I opened my eyes, I was alone. The stench from the sink brought my attention back to the mess in front of me. Using it as an excuse, I ran the water and cleaned what I could with some hand towels. When it looked clean, I splashed cold water over my face and rinsed out my mouth, desperately wanting to go and brush my teeth.

Back in the main clubhouse, I stood for a second and breathed through my mouth as my nose continued to burn, pulling myself together. Weakness was not something I liked to reveal to anyone. I'd learned that it was only exploited.

Rolling my shoulders, I walked back into church. Linc raised one brow, and I nodded before returning to my seat. The conversation that had been going on ceased as I sat. It was then I noticed Toad wasn't in the room. "Where's Toad?"

"He went after you."

"He came into the restroom then left." Even as I answered, I searched the room, the sinking feeling gnawing at my raw stomach increasing with every second. Had he gone to use the other restroom?

Getting to my feet, I headed back into the empty club. My gaze swept the room as I headed through it. The sound of folks moving behind me was ignored as I went from room to room. Where the fuck had he gone? He couldn't leave without me. Had he gone out for some air?

Out the main door, my heart hammered hard against my ribs at the lack of any sign of Toad in the dim evening light. The sound of insects buzzing competed with the buzz in my ears.

"Where'd he go?" Linc growled.

"I don't fucking know. It's not like him. Did we push him too hard?" Had I pushed him into a corner and he got scared?

"I got a bad feeling about this," Ram said as he appeared next to Linc.

"Search the building. Mason will be back in the apartment, so check with him. Maybe Toad's there."

A ray of hope bloomed in my chest as I took off before anyone else could move. Please let him be with Mason, please.

I didn't knock as I burst into Linc's apartment. Mason was sitting at the large table with a computer, and his head popped up with a frown. "What, has something happened to Linc?" He didn't finish speaking before he was up and on his feet.

Linc appeared behind me, and Mason looked visibly relieved.

"It's Toad. Have you seen him?" I snarled, too scared for pleasantries right then.

Mason shook his head. "Not since I left the meeting." He glanced at Linc, a spark of anger still there in his eyes.

Linc's eyes hardened. "We'll talk about that later. Toad has disappeared."

"Did he leave in a cab? I thought I heard a car a few minutes ago. I can't be sure."

A throbbing ache started to develop behind my eyes. "But you think?"

The nod was measured. "I would say I heard a vehicle of some sort. It's quiet out here, and it's not like you hear cars out here often."

"Call his phone," Linc demanded.

My hand was already reaching into the back of my jeans. Seconds later, I was back to having a stomach that hated me. "It's switched off. Would he do that? Would he turn off his phone?" Each question was making me sicker. It was a struggle to keep standing as Linc's expression didn't quite hide his concern.

I blew out a hard breath. "Do you think..." I couldn't say it.

The room became crowded with members, the noise level making it hard to think. Not that I wanted to right then.

"Everyone, calm down," Mason stated in a stern voice that carried around the room. "We need to be level-headed about this. If this has anything to do with Toad's past and not that he's just dropped his phone and broken it, then we need to think about our next move."

I didn't miss how he included himself in figuring out the next move.

"Ram, can you ring around the cab companies that are local and see if Toad called to get picked up at this address. Sid, head back to the auto shop and see if Toad went back there. Razor, you own two of the gas stations locally. Can you check to see if anyone has filled up for gas that stood out?"

I didn't hear the rest. I was already heading out the door. At my bike, the sight of Toad's helmet hanging off my handlebar was enough to buckle my legs. Get a fucking grip.

I used the stern voice in my head to keep me from focusing too hard on the panic that wanted to snatch away any level of calm I might have. On the motorcycle, I rode like the devil himself was chasing me. It seemed like an eternity by the time I arrived at the auto shop. One look at the darkened windows and I sensed the place was empty. I parked the bike then went through the motions of going up to the apartment to check every room.

Nothing! Nothing!

Where the fuck was he?

Chapter 14

TOAD

I'd gone, albeit reluctantly, to find Sid. I didn't want to face his judgment on things I couldn't change. Things I'd done to survive, to eat, to have a roof over my head. The shame I pushed to the back of my mind had surfaced when Sid had disappeared out of the room.

In the restroom, the distress on Sid's face was too much to bear, so I did what I always do, I ran through the main room, avoiding going back to church. I needed space for my head, for my heart to decide what I needed to do.

The muggy air was a warm relief after the iciness that had formed inside me at having to open up wounds and reveal them. There'd been sympathy, anger, disgust, and many other emotions, but thankfully, they hadn't been aimed at me, more the situation I'd been in. That was until I'd answered the last question without thinking about my answer. All I could see was Sid's face in front of me.

The anger blocked out everything else. Linc had encouraged me to go after Sid as if understanding there was something more between us.

He couldn't even bear to look at me.

Never a smoker, right then I wished I was because I needed the distraction, something to stop me from going back in and...what, I wasn't sure. But whatever it was, I needed it to be convincing so that Sid realized what I felt for him was real. I'd never have spoken about my past if it weren't for him. Did he even get that?

In all the years I'd been on the run from my past, I'd never gotten so lost in my thoughts that someone could creep up on me. My heart skipped a beat as I was too late to register the sound of soft footfalls before two figures appeared as if from nowhere. I spun around, my mouth opening as something pierced at my neck.

"What the fuckkkkk?" The drug was fast-acting. I could feel it weaving quickly through my body with each beat of my heart. It stole my ability to do more than slur my words as my legs buckled under me. Expecting to hit the ground hard, large, unforgiving arms clasped hold. The huge, muscled arm cut off my ability to breathe properly. The world tipped, then I was being carried. My mouth wouldn't work. My lips felt as numb as my body.

The effects of the drug worked to slow down my thoughts, though it didn't stop the reality from dawning that what I'd been running from had finally caught up with me.

A lone tear fell to the ground unheeded as I was thrown into the back of a vehicle. My mind too sluggish to do more than register the loss of Sid, of my brothers.

There was the sound of voices, but I couldn't make out what it was they were saying as I slipped deeper into a drug-induced numbness. One I was awfully familiar with, one that they knew would keep me from fighting back.

💀 💀 💀

Awareness seeped back in, and it was a struggle to remain still as the drugs started to wear off. The engine purred beneath me as the world came back into focus. The dimness in the car and the fact that I was lying on the back seat made it impossible to see who was in the front of the car. Neither man's face had been my priority until they'd jabbed me with whatever they'd given me.

Had I been out of it long? I strained my neck to see if I could catch anything out of the window above my head. I swallowed the sigh of frustration when all I could see was the darkening sky. Had the club members realized I was gone? Fuck! Would

Sid think I'd fucked off on my own? An ache developed in my chest at the thought of him thinking I'd just leave without saying anything.

He wouldn't believe that, not after what we'd shared. Would he?

It was a toss-up after seeing the vomit in the sink in front of him earlier.

"Did you throw his phone away?"

I held my breath at the sound of the unfamiliar voice, not wanting to alert them to the fact I was awake and alert enough to move. Although it was harder than I'd liked because of the urge to check my pocket for my phone. At the other guy's response, my heart flipped in my chest.

"I'm not a fucking moron. I switched it off and threw it into the undergrowth. No fucker will find it, or him. How long have we got before we need to stick him again?"

The first dude answered, "Midazolam is what they gave us, and it only lasts about an hour or so, I think. They said it causes memory loss, so he won't be able to remember a thing. Not that that is the point here." He sounded so fucking blasé as if he were talking about the weather, giving me the urge to punch him in the throat.

Years of suppressed anger that I'd worked to control in order to try to fit in and conform bubbled up inside me. The years I'd been free, I'd learned to fight, to stand up for myself. If these motherfuckers thought I was going to go down without a fight, then they were going to be sadly mistaken. I just needed to avoid the stabby things full of drugs.

"We need gas. Did we pass any places in this godforsaken hole?"

"There was one on the edge of town near the interstate for Killeen. Stop there. I need to piss. We can grab some snacks. It's a long-ass trip back."

As they continued to talk, my heart rate skyrocketed when I realized we'd only been in the car for about twenty minutes. The drugs clearly didn't last as long as they'd hoped for. I carefully moved my arms and legs. Once more keeping silent at the relief that followed that they hadn't bothered to restrain me. Their stupidity hopefully would continue to work in my favor. Then something tickled at the edge of my memory. Did Razor own the gas station at the edge of town? He owned a couple, but I couldn't remember which ones he'd said were his.

The conversation stopped, and I worked to keep my breathing even so it looked like I was still out of it. Would they leave me in the car alone? I didn't have to wait too long to find out as minutes later, lights flashed in the car as it slowed to a stop. I could see the overhanging roof of the gas station.

I shut my eyes when the first dude asked. "Is he covered in the back?"

"The darkened windows should stop anyone seeing him. And if they do, he just looks like he's asleep."

"I'll stay here. You take a piss, then grab some food. I'll get the gas when you're done."

Shit!

One is better than two. I argued with myself as I kept still at the sound of the door on my right being opened and slammed shut. Working on keeping my breathing even, I counted to twenty before I slowly shifted to sit up behind the guy looking down at something in his hand. Working on instinct, I sat up, not making any noise because I wanted to keep the element of surprise. The guy was by no means small, but with the level of anger running wild inside me, I wasn't worried. I pressed my front to the back of his seat. At the same time, I wrapped my arms around the headrest and clasped my hands together. In the split-second it took for him to make a startled sound, I pulled back hard against his throat and held him in a chokehold. Any residual pain in my left hand was pushed to the back of my mind as the dude started to thrash around in the seat.

Grunts filled the car as we struggled together. He tried to lurch forward, back braced against his seat, but he had nowhere to go. Fingers dug ruthlessly into the back of my exposed hand. The bandage helped to take some of the assault off it while he gouged at me. Don't let go, don't let fucking go.

On repeat, I slammed my eyes shut and pressed as hard as I could against his throat, hoping to cut off his air supply. Gritting my teeth, I held on, knowing this was my life I was fighting for. Unsure how long we struggled, sweat dripped down the sides of my face and I was starting to lose strength. In a last-ditch attempt, I twisted my hand a little to push my thumb deep into his windpipe and started to pray the fucker would just give up.

Breathless and feeling waves of dizziness wash over me, I cursed whatever they'd used on me as I felt my grip losing traction. Was he getting weaker? "Fucker, pass the fuck out," I growled, trying to catch my breath and get a better grip. The years of rage, of fear, pushed at me, along with what they'd steal from me if they took me again: Sid.

It took a second to notice the guy had stopped fighting and his hands were motionless on mine. Was it a trick? The thought left me pressing harder for a few more seconds, squeezing fiercely as my arms shook violently. The guy didn't make any sounds, nothing.

Chest heaving, I released him slowly. My arms ached, and my hand was throbbing as I shifted back to tilt my head to the side and glance out the front window. The thumping inside my skull left me deafened as I saw a guy dressed in black at the counter inside the gas station's convenience store and no one else in the small shop. The guy's attention was on the cashier.

One glance over the seat at the unconscious guy, I swallowed to wet my throat. Taking several deep breaths, I sank down in the seat and opened the door, all but crawling out on my hands and knees. I carefully shoved the door too to make it look as if it was closed. Still on my hands and knees, I used the car as a barrier as I glanced about, looking for something to hide behind.

Shit! Fuck!

Nothing, not a car or a fucking bush between me and the line of trees that separated the lot from the houses behind. There was no way the guy wouldn't miss me if he looked out the window. I debated for another second. There were no sounds of traffic, no one coming to my rescue. I was on my own like I'd always been. My head dipped between my shoulders. Stop the fucking self-pity and fucking move.

Taking a deep breath, I got up, my legs wavering along with my vision. Allowing myself only a second to gather courage, I was off and running. The noise of my boots hitting the ground sounded loud as the adrenaline burst gave me the energy I needed to speed up. With each passing second, I expected there to be the sound of a shout or even a car engine. When I reached the tree line, I threw a quick glance over my shoulder and stumbled as my foot hit a thick root. I careened forward, propelled into a large tree. Weakness in my arms left them heavy, and my reaction wasn't quick enough as my head collided with the tree. Pain exploded behind my eyes as the world once again disappeared before I could curse my shitty luck.

Chapter 15

SID

As the minutes ticked by, the panic eating at my guts turned ravenous, keeping me pacing outside the back of the auto shop, waiting for someone to call me, anyone. Linc had been clear I was to wait here and not go off on a mad tear around town. It was fucking hard to do with the image of what Toad had already endured at his parents' hands. In all my years, I'd never felt this out of control. I wasn't sure what I'd do if anything happened to Toad.

The fucker had burrowed past my defenses. I just hadn't realized how much until it hit that I might have lost my chance to try, and…

The night sounds disappeared with the ringing of my phone. Razor's name flashed up, and my heart went crazy, attempting to leave my chest as I answered. "Anything?" The air remained stuck somewhere inside me as I waited for him to reply.

"Rory called to say a car with Washington State plates on it just pulled in for gas. He's going to keep the guys occupied until we get there. He's at the gas station on the edge of town."

I exhaled noisily. "Can he see Toad?"

"Nope, he said only two big dudes in the front of the car. But if they've taken him, then they ain't gonna leave him on show, are they?" Razor bit out.

It was too much of a coincidence that the plates were from where Toad's family was located. It had to be them who'd taken Toad. I wasn't going to contemplate anything else right then with my instincts kicking in.

"I'm on my way." I hit End Call and shoved my cell phone into my jacket. The twenty questions my head wanted answers for were shut down before they got the better of me. On my hog, I switched on the engine. The roar as I took off was deafening for a few seconds as gravel spat everywhere. I exited the parking lot without checking for other vehicles. Right then, I had one priority—find Toad.

A sense of dread I didn't want to acknowledge, swirled in my already raw stomach that I might not find Toad in the car. There was no doubt he'd been taken by someone when I'd seen his bike sitting in the auto shop, where I'd put it for him. He'd never leave without it. He might go without his personal things, but he'd never leave his hog. It was the first piece he told me he'd worked on and the one he was most proud of.

Sweat slid unpleasantly down my back as I blinked repeatedly, trying to swallow past the ball lodged in my throat. The gas station was minutes away from the auto shop. It still felt like forever to get there. When the lights of the gas station appeared in front of me, I slowed. There was no sign of any of the other Dark Angels. I hadn't needed to ask Razor if he'd called the other members. It was a given.

The sight of the lone car made the decision for me. The sound of my engine would alert Toad, if he was conscious and in the car, that someone was coming for him. I parked right in front of the car, seeing the pump they'd used was the one that was hard to reverse out of. As I swung my leg off my hog, I glanced into the car.

The guy in the driver's seat had his head bowed forward as if he were sleeping. Would a dude fall asleep if they'd just kidnapped someone? Anxiety roamed freely through me as I glanced into the shop at Rory, who was having a heated discussion with a large guy dressed all in black.

The guy was scowling and pointing at the card machine on the counter. I sucked in a shaky breath and walked to the large Cadillac. The windows were blacked out, making it impossible for me to see the backseat. As I got closer, I noticed that one of the back seat doors was open.

Hands slick with sweat, I reached for the door as I looked back at the dude in the front seat. He remained slouched and unmoving. Had something happened to him?

As I slowly pulled open the door, my stomach flipped and dove for the ground as it landed on what sat on the floor. There, behind the driver's seat, was a dirty bandage. One I'd put on Toad that morning, I was positive of it. The smear of grease I'd gotten on it when Toad had come into the auto shop to check what he had booked in the following month was right there taunting me.

Where the fuck was he?

"Who the fuck are you? And what are you doing in my car?" came an angry shout as the man who'd been inside, moments ago, ran toward me. His eyes were firing all sorts of warnings that I didn't give two fucks about right then.

Behind him, Rory waved at me and lifted one finger. I didn't acknowledge the message that my brothers were a minute away. I was already preparing for what was coming. I wanted answers, and I wanted them now. I didn't care how I got them.

The guy faltered a couple of feet from the car, his gaze shifting to the interior. It struck me then that the other dude hadn't gotten out of the car. Had he not heard the shouting?

"What have you done to Craig?" The guy was back to sounding outraged, and if I wasn't mistaken, there was fear too.

148

I stood to my full height and growled. "Where is Toad?"

That only got a confused reaction as the guy frowned, his gaze repeatedly shifting between me and the front of the car, tension rolling off him. A sheen of sweat appeared on the dude's forehead.

It registered they wouldn't know Toad's nickname. "Mark Wyatt, what did you do with him?"

That got an instant reaction, and his gaze moved to the open door at the rear of the car I'd stepped away from.

"Don't know who that is or what the fuck this is all about." His hand moved toward his jacket pocket.

"Keep still, dickweed."

He didn't listen, his lips moving into a sneer. That was his second mistake. The first was taking something precious to me. I lunged hard and fast, using my body weight to shove him so hard it lifted him clear off the ground.

He landed hard enough to rattle every bone in his body. "Fuckerrrrrrr," he bellowed, pain etched into his face. I didn't give him a chance to get up as I jumped on him and pinned him to the ground, giving him two solid punches to his stomach while I pressed one knee into his groin, then lay my forearm over his neck. It was then I heard the sounds of my brothers coming.

The roar of the engines calmed me as I pressed harder against his windpipe, a feral smile spreading over my face. "You ever imagine what Hell looks like?" The guy struggled, but he was no match against me. His face went an ugly shade of purple as I whispered next to his ear, "'Cause you're about to find out."

"The dude in the car is out cold. Do you think Toad did that?" Rory asked as he came into my line of sight.

"Let's fucking hope. Can you grab something to tie these pair of fuckers up with?" I didn't take my eyes off the dude under me who was trying to buck me off. I pressed my knee snuggly against his groin until he got the point.

Motorcycles circled the car and me as, one by one, the engines died. My chest swelled with pride that I had brothers to cover my back.

Linc crouched in front of me and placed his hand on the guy's forehead but looked at me. "You sure these dudes are the ones who took Toad?"

"Yep, there's a bandage in the back of the car. It's the one I put on his hand this morning. There ain't no sign of Toad. Rory says the guy in the driver's seat is out cold."

As I spoke, Ram dragged the other guy out of the car. His head lolled to the side to reveal dark bruising to his throat. He pressed his fingers to the side of his neck for a few seconds. "Yep, out cold."

The guy under me went stiff as a board, his gaze showing real fear as it returned to me.

"I'm tellin' you now. If there is one hair harmed on Toad's head, you'll understand what pain really fuckin' is."

"Where is he?" Linc gritted out.

Lifting my arm, the guy rasped defeatedly, "He was in the back of the car."

Linc bitch-slapped him, his head bouncing off the asphalt. "Wrong fuckin' answer." Linc stood and motioned for everyone to come closer. "Search this area first. Toad can't have gone far as he's on foot and possibly injured. If he's not around these parts, start searching the streets. I want him found."

Quick discussions followed before folks took off. Wanting to help, I eyed Linc as Rory returned with several long bits of rope. "Can you take over? I wanna help search."

After a curt nod, I gave the guy a warning glare. "I wouldn't try anything if you want to walk again." With that, I got up, waiting for Linc to grab the fucker before I turned to look around. It was then I saw Tina disappear into the line of trees at the edge of the lot. This was followed by a loud cry. "Here, help me." I was running before she'd finished shouting.

If there's a God, let him be okay.

I crashed through the tree line and came to an abrupt stop at the sight of Toad's bloody and battered face. I dropped to my knees at the side of him, reaching out to touch his neck with trembling fingers.

"He's breathin', but this cut is bleedin' like a bitch," Tina muttered distractedly as she dug into her jacket pocket and pulled out a scarf she wore over her lower face when on her motorcycle. She pressed it to Toad's head while I looked on helplessly.

Tina nudged my arm. "Call for a goddamn ambulance. He needs someone to look at his head."

Jarred from my misery, I did as she asked, my gaze never leaving Toad.

By the time I'd finished talking on the phone, other club members had appeared. I glanced toward Razor. "You need to get those men and car out of here and back to the clubhouse. You can't afford for the sheriff to be stickin' his nose in our business. Tell Linc that once I know Toad is safe, I'll come to the clubhouse."

"Will do. I'll send Mel to relieve you so someone stays with Toad." I nodded.

As quickly as everyone had arrived, they disappeared. I didn't need to check that they'd do as I asked as I waited for the truck to arrive with Tina.

Chapter 16

The unmistakable scent of a hospital sank past the layer of pain in my head. I willed my body to behave and not react. Had they found me? Was I back in...hell?

Working to keep my breathing deep and even, I twitched my fingers, feeling the weight of the cover touching my skin. With care, I lifted first one hand then the other hand. No restraints! That had to be good. Or were they trying to fool me?

"Where do you think the doc's at? That nurse said they'd be back with the results of the tests they took. It's been fuckin' ages!" Sid growled.

"Keep it down. You don't wanna get us kicked out. You already made a fuss," Tina replied, sounding as pissed as Sid.

I slit open my eyes, mindful of the pain. "Where am I?" I rasped past the dryness in my throat.

"Thank fuck!" Sid's face appeared above me, and my heart stopped for a second as I studied his face. The grim lines etched deep into his features left me with a wild fluttering feeling in the center of my chest.

"How long have I been out?"

The hand he placed on my cheek shook as his Adam's apple bobbed repeatedly. "A day. It's Saturday night."

I shut my eyes and blew out a breath as the worry returned. "My family."

"Are going to be dealt with," Sid ground out, not letting me finish.

Lifting my eyelids took effort, but I did it to make sure Sid was looking at me when I spoke. "You promised me. Don't do this. You have no clue what they're capable of. Think about it, those two goons found me because my name, only in part, was entered into a goddamn computer system here in this hospital. I've been here a day. If you gave them my name, they'll already know I'm here. They'll know what injuries I have, fuck they'll probably know what color underwear I have on. Don't you get it?" Sid's expression turned grimmer if it was at all possible, but he remained silent until I had finished.

His fingers were gentle as he lowered his face until we were mere inches apart. "Do you have any

154

idea how fucked up I was to find you gone?" His voice was deadly soft. "How lucky those two fuckers are that I'm here with you and not at the clubhouse?"

I struggled to sit up, but Sid shook his head and pushed my shoulder against the bed. "You're not movin' until the doc clears you."

"Those men—"

"Will be dealt with. Right now that's not what's important."

"How can you say that?" I gritted out, fast losing my patience, which wasn't helping the jackhammer trying to drill through my skull.

"'Cause I can. Now lie back, and we'll talk about this after the doc clears you." His jaw flexed as he kept his hard stare directed at me until I did as he said.

He released my shoulder as I sank into the mattress, too tired to fight right then as the aches and pains in my body made their presence known. I lifted my left hand when I realized it wasn't bandaged.

"They left it uncovered and stuck some gunk on it when they were treatin' you in the ER. The plastic surgeon came by and took a look at your hand. He said somethin' 'bout it healin' fast, and you don't need a bandage anymore," Tina said, coming to the side of the bed and giving me a tight smile.

She glanced at Sid, and he stepped back to take the seat she'd just vacated.

One look at her tired face, and I understood that they had stayed with me. A tightness developed in my chest at the reality they'd watched over me. "Thanks for staying."

"No problem, kiddo." She got a little closer and, in a stage-whisper, said, "It was either here with Sid or go and look at Razor's ugly face. It was a tough call."

I laughed, then winced, regretting it as the pain worsened.

"You're a laugh a minute," Sid muttered, not looking at either of us as he slouched in the chair, his eyes drifting shut.

"Did you get any sleep?" I asked Tina while keeping my gaze on Sid.

"Nope. We were on guard duty." She shrugged and gave my arm a gentle pat. "You'll learn we take all our members' safety seriously."

The door opening got Sid sitting back up, instantly alert.

The nurse who appeared looked like a dear caught in headlights as she stared at Sid for longer than was necessary before she looked at me. "Oh, you're awake. That's great. The doctor is just starting his evening rounds."

Sid stood and walked to the side of the bed. "What about the test results you were supposed to be discussin' with us?"

"Yes, the doctor will discuss those with Mr. Thomas now that he's awake," she answered.

Thomas? Who the fuck was Mr. Thomas? My lips parted, and Sid pressed his hand down on my leg in a move I recognized was meant to keep me quiet. Firming my mouth, I gave him a hard stare as the nurse continued talking about how long it might take for the doctor to reach my room.

When she left a minute later, I asked, "Mr. Thomas? Who's that?"

"You, you dumb fool," Sid answered, a scowl forming on his face as he glanced at Tina. "After the doc's been in, you can head out. I'll stay here."

"Don't I get a say in this?"

Both Tina and Sid answered, "No" before they carried on talking like I wasn't in the room.

"Ok, you don't want someone to switch with you? You've been up thirty-six hours, give or take."

"It's fine. I'll catch some shut-eye in the chair."

The conversation stopped when, a second later, the door opened again to reveal a woman dressed in navy scrubs with a stethoscope hanging around her neck. I gauged her age to be somewhere from mid-forties to early fifties due to the salt-and-pepper hair cropped into a short style that suited her small face.

Intelligent eyes moved from me to Tina and Sid. "I'm Dr. Swann. I'm the doctor in charge tonight of the ICU How are you feeling, Mr. Thomas?"

It took a second to register that she was talking to me. "I could do with something to take the edge off the pain in my head. Otherwise, I'm good, ready to get out of here." I injected enthusiasm into my voice that I wasn't feeling, hoping it would get me out of this place.

"Let's have a look at you, and then we'll talk about the next steps."

Sid and Tina, in unison, stepped back from the bed as the doctor approached and the same nurse who'd been in minutes earlier came back, shutting the door behind her. She stood to the side, saying nothing.

Dr. Swann asked several questions to check my memory. Things like what month it was, the year, and the date. Sid fidgeted as she pulled the stethoscope from her neck and started to examine me. She pulled what looked like a pen out of her pocket when she finished listening to my chest. "I'm going to shine a light in your eyes. If it causes you pain, just let me know, and I'll stop."

"He said he was in pain. Can't you give him something before you do that shit?" Sid growled, coming closer to the bed, an intimidating scowl appearing.

The doctor nodded at Sid. "You are correct." She glanced back at the nurse. "Can you bring his drug chart so I can see what we can give Mr. Thomas?"

There was a little back and forth when she returned with it, and my pain level was discussed. All I wanted was the drugs and to go home with Sid and hide from the world for a bit.

Pills swallowed with some water five minutes later, the doctor perched on the edge of the bed. "The scan we did of your head shows no swelling or acute injury. That being said, you've been unconscious for over twenty- four hours, making me a little cautious about discharging you too soon."

"Sorry, doc, but I ain't stayin' if there isn't anything wrong with the scan results. I'm better off at home."

"I disagree. You need to be observed for at least another twenty-four to forty-eight hours in a hospital." Her voice was stern, but her face was sympathetic.

I was already shaking my head. The wince was hard to disguise, with the pain pills not having any effect yet. "Sid will be there if I need anything." I gave him an imploring look, hoping that he'd agree.

His expression gave nothing away as it shifted from me to the doctor. "What would I need to be watchin' out for?"

I didn't breathe easy as the doctor shook her head. "Do you plan on staying at his side for the next two days? Because that's what he'll need."

"No one is going to be in here with me all the time," I argued.

Sternness came off her in big fucking waves as she stood. "That might be the case, but right outside that door is the best medical equipment and experienced staff who can help if you should deteriorate."

It was hard to argue back, and my heart sank at the reality it was a losing battle. There was no way Sid would want to be with me for twenty-four hours, never mind forty-eight.

Sid's body stiffened. "The hospital is ten minutes from my apartment. Do you think I have anything to worry about if I take him home?"

Was he going to watch over me?

Mixed emotions coursed through me, but the prominent one was relief that he'd do this for me. I worked to try and not pin my hopes on him after what he'd said when I'd woken, but it was harder than I liked with him giving me what I wanted.

"Would you consider spending the night and letting me review you in the morning? Is that a compromise you're willing to accept? You've only just recovered consciousness. Safety-wise, you'd be better off here for at least one night." Her tone turned cajoling, and I could see the moment Sid accepted that even before he looked at me.

"One night, and I'll take you home in the morning."

There was no give in his stony expression. I released an exasperated sigh. "Tonight, that's it, and I get to leave first thing in the morning." I glanced at Dr. Swann. "You'll come and see me first, right? No fuckin' about, no delays."

Her lips twitched, but she showed no other signs of finding my comments amusing. "Yes, I'll come and see you first."

She finished her examination, and she was right. The flashlight being shined into my eyes wasn't in my top ten of pleasant things to experience. After she left with one more promise I'd see her early in the morning, I closed my eyes and shut out Sid, who I was more than a little pissed at. Although I knew he was only doing what he thought was best.

"You go, Tina. I'll be fine here."

"You sure? You want me to go and get you something to eat? The food in here is shit," Tina offered.

There was the sound of something scraping over the floor before Sid answered, "Nope, I ain't hungry. I'm just gonna catch some shut-eye."

There was more noise as the door opened then shut, followed by muted sounds out in the hallway. I lay and waited for Sid to say something. As the time stretched and he remained silent, I pried open my sore eyes. The scraping now made sense as Sid sat slumped in the seat now next to my bed. His face was relaxed and his breathing even. It appeared he'd fallen asleep, and it gave me the first opportunity to look at his unguarded face.

It struck how closed off he was, that the mask was there to protect against revealing that underneath was a person with a tender heart. He'd kick my ass for thinking it, but he had a big heart just like me. The difference was his had been hit way too many times, and whereas I'd never given up the hope that I'd find someone to love me regardless of the past, he had. I must be sick because, fuck, if anything it made me want it more.

Sid's words came back to me, "Do you have any idea how fucked up I was to find you gone?" What did they mean? Was he fucked up as in pissed off? Or was it something else? Did he have the same feelings for me as I had for him?

He stirred and moved as if to get a little more comfortable. In the small seat, that was going to be impossible, but he settled again, his eyes remaining closed. He wasn't quite close enough for me to reach out and touch, but he was close enough that I let my eyes drift closed as the drugs started to kick in. For the first time in my life, I felt...safe in a hospital.

Chapter 17

SID

As promised, the doc came and gave Toad her consent to leave the following morning, with strict instructions to return if he had any problems with headaches or his vision.

Tina had one of the guys drop the auto shop truck off and get them to leave the keys at the reception desk. Toad refused a wheelchair to take him to the entrance, and I didn't argue with him. His face was a sight; the bruises that started at the center of his forehead where the gash was came down like a ghoulish mask of dark colors. Both eyes were black, the swelling had gone down some, but he still looked like he'd been on the receiving end of a beatdown.

Heads turned as we walked through the hallways. Toad hunched his shoulders, his gaze firmly fixed on the ground. With Toad scowling at anyone who chose to look at us, a few people hurried past. By the time we got to the exit, Toad was back to his head doing the weird bobbing thing as he glanced around the parking lot.

"We gave a fake name. They don't know you're here."

He didn't pause as he answered, "You don't know that for sure."

I waited till we got back into the truck before I replied, "I do. We're careful. We have separate IDs for all members, just in case. If you'd been upfront from the start, I'd have used it the first time you ended up in this joint."

His eyes widened. "No one's ever mentioned this at the club."

"That's 'cause we keep it on the down-low. Members are normally a little more forthcomin' in sharin' their shit with us." I struggled to keep my frustration to myself.

He sighed while rubbing at his tender face with his now unbandaged hand. "Yeah, okay. Do we need to get into this now? I can't go back and change things."

The defeated posture as he faced forward did little to help with all the mixed feelings that had been riding my ass hard from the moment he'd been snatched. The twenty-four hours he'd lain motionless in the bed, barely looking like he was breathing, had to have been some of the worst of my life. And I'd had some hideous fucking moments to compare them to. It was terrifying how much this man had come to mean to me. How much he'd managed to get under my defenses. I'd nearly confessed as much and had only at the last second remembered Tina was still in the room when Toad had woken.

"Let's get you back to the apartment."

He stiffened before he glanced back at me. "No. Where are the two shitheads that took me?"

I chuckled, and Toad shivered next to me. "On ice."

The alarm in his wide eyes was comical. "What's that supposed to mean?"

"Exactly what I said, on ice. The cooler. It's out back of the bar. There is a cellar that came courtesy of Linc's granddaddy. When the place was wrecked a few years back, Linc found the cellar when they re-built. It was still intact. The place is fuckin' bombproof. The old-timers had forgotten all about it as it hadn't been used in decades. It was where Linc's granddaddy made illegal liquor to sell. Linc kept it, seeing it as a sign that it was the only part that was still whole after the hurricane." I chuckled. "It's called the cooler because the place never gets warm."

He nodded, though the worry lines didn't disappear. "Then take me there. I need to figure out what my parents wanted. When I came to in the back of the car, the way they were talkin', I wasn't sure whether they'd come to get rid of me rather than take me back."

Each word stabbed at the center of me. "You sure?"

He winced. "Not one hundred percent, no. They gave me somethin' they said takes my memories."

"Then I'll take you to the clubhouse." I put the truck in drive and took off. Linc had been quiet about what, if anything, they'd done to the two guys. We were always careful about what went into a message if we had the sheriff's department wanting to give us crap for any reason.

The ride was silent, and I left Toad to his thoughts as he stared out the side window rubbing at his left hand that was, in their eyes, healed enough not to require anything other than the ointments to keep the skin from tightening. It looked ten times better than it had. Did this mean Toad would want to go back to his own apartment now he didn't need me?

I shoved the thought away, not liking how I got a sinking feeling at him leaving my home as I pulled into the dirt road that led to the club. There were motorcycles parked out front, Linc's one of them, showing he'd spent the night. Was Mason here? The guy had been solid in the past, but would what was about to go down be a step too far? Mason was all about playing it straight and legal. He wasn't one for overstepping into the gray. Linc straddled that line, and I understood it was probably harder on him now that he had Mason in his life.

Toad got out of the truck wordlessly, not waiting for me. He was up the porch steps and inside the clubhouse before I'd turned off the engine and gotten out of the cab. At a slower pace, I went after him. In the clubhouse, Matt, Razor, and Ram were sitting at the bar with Linc. There was no sign of Mason or River.

My gaze tracked to where Toad was standing, his face showing his agitation as he motioned to Linc. "Have they said anything?"

Linc shook his head. "They haven't had the chance." The chuckle that followed was dark and dangerous. "I was waitin' for you to get started."

Ram cracked his knuckles while Matt's eyes showed malicious intent.

Razor stood. "We gonna do this down in the cooler or up here?"

"Out back. I don't wanna have any blood evidence inside this building," Linc answered as he followed suit and stood, his gaze moving to each man. "It goes without sayin' that none of this gets discussed in front of Mason."

I frowned. "Does he know the guys are here?"

Linc gave a curt nod. "He does. He wants to...do things legal like. We'll do that, but only after we've had words with them. Only thing, don't mark them anywhere obvious."

Once everyone gave their agreement, Razor and Linc disappeared out the back. I glanced at Toad. "You up for this?"

He visibly bristled, but I didn't care if he was insulted. Right then, all I wanted was to keep him...safe. He narrowed the distance between us as Matt and Ram disappeared out the back door behind the bar.

"You think I can't hold my own?" he growled low and menacing.

"I think you just woke the fuck up after bashing your head. That's what I think."

"Yeah, I'll give you that. But before I knocked myself out cold, I put down one of those big fuckers on my own."

The anger directed at me left no option if I didn't want to get into it with him without pushing back. "Point taken," I conceded.

"Then let's get on with this." He spun on his heel to head around the bar and out the door.

I hated to admit to myself how much I wanted to keep him out of harm's way right then, so I went after him, taking several deep breaths to prepare for what was coming.

As I stepped out the back, the two men were dragged from the inconspicuous door that looked more like part of the undergrowth. Inspecting them, they both looked like they'd be able to hold their own in a fight. The larger one bore marks around his neck where Toad had held him in a chokehold. His eyes held dark anger as they landed on Toad, causing me to take a step closer to Toad.

He didn't acknowledge the move, but I was sure he hadn't missed it, and neither had Linc, whose brows arched at me.

"What's this, the welcoming committee?" he bigger of the two said in a low growl.

Before anyone could respond, Toad was on him, tackling him to the ground, nearly taking Linc off his feet with the force. Any thoughts I'd had that Toad would struggle fled as the huge guy landed hard enough that I felt the earth under my boots move. They hit the ground with Toad landing on top, his forearm crushing the guy's throat. "No, we're the fucking death squad if you don't start explainin' who the fuck sent you and what you were plannin' on doin'," Toad snapped.

The guy held by Razor struggled for a second until Linc gave him a solid punch to the gut. He doubled over, going down to his knees, and spat on the ground as he gasped for breath. Linc yanked on the dude's hair pulling his head back. "Talk. I won't ask twice."

The guy spat again as his gaze shifted to his partner in crime, who was starting to look a dark shade of purple as his eyes bulged. Toad didn't seem inclined to let up the pressure as he took one knee and pressed hard down on the guy's balls, making me wince.

"The Hanna's employed us to collect their son. They weren't after him returnin' home but taken to a remote location where he could be housed."

I didn't miss the shudder Toad gave at the answer. "That ain't happenin', not in this lifetime or any other." I crouched next to the dude Toad had a hold of. I made sure he was looking directly at me so he could see I was deadly serious. "I'm going to say this only once, so listen up. You'll get to go back to the Hanna's, and I want you to give them a message from Dark Angels. If they so much as step in Toad's direction, sniff the fuckin' air he breathes, then none of their money or political bullshit crap will protect them from what's coming for them."

Toad looked me dead in the eye with something akin to worship that I'd need to think about later when I was alone. "You finished with this scumbag?"

His answer was to release the guy's throat. His knee lifted, and the guy didn't have a chance to take a breath when Toad brought it back down hard enough to draw winces from those of us watching.

"Arghhhhhhh," the dude called out, reaching for his balls.

Toad got up, not paying the guy any attention as the dude rolled to his side, bringing his knees up into his body.

"I'm done now," Toad gritted out, then walked back into the clubhouse, not looking back.

Chapter 18

TOAD

Shaking and trying not to show it, I walked through the back door of the clubhouse and leaned against the wall once I was out of sight. The urge to puke left my mouth watering as I tried to swallow back the bile that was burning my throat.

Sid's warning had done all sorts of things to my heart, but it didn't stop what I knew was going to be coming our way. My family wasn't good with threats. That left me with two options, run or stay and fight. My whole life, I'd run. Run from standing up to the fuckers, run from the place they'd put me, and I was still running. Was it time to stop and see where the cards fell?

I rubbed at the center of my chest at the ache that came from the knowledge this was no longer just about me. This was about Sid, about my brothers. Could they survive the reach of my family and walk away unscathed? The image of little River playing on the front porch ran through my head and icy dread followed.

A family with no morals, I understood, would use anything to get what they wanted. Would they try and use River? Breathless at the answer, I sagged against the wall in defeat. *Run. You need to run!*

As if I'd transmitted the doom and gloom now filling my head, Linc appeared through the door on my left.

His dark features highlighted just why he was named Killer. His gaze swept over me, and he shook his head. "We'll deal with the fallout, whatever it is."

"You don't know what they're capable of. They'll aim at our weak spots." I sucked in a shaky breath. "At River," I whispered.

Linc tensed, but his expression never changed. "If we know what's coming, then we'll be ready. They won't get anywhere near River. Mason will make sure of that." His voice was full of confidence, which I wasn't feeling, but I didn't argue. "We're brothers, family. Each and every person will fight for you. Will stand for you. Will you do the same and stay?"

He'd laid it out, left me no place to go as lying was never going to be an option, and he knew it. I released the breath that had gotten caught in my chest. "Yes, I'll stay and stand with my brothers."

The nod from Linc was followed by a hand to my shoulder. "Thanks for the honesty." He walked off, going across the room and out the main door.

I debated going back to see what was going on outside, but I was too damn tired to do more than stagger to one of the leather chairs and sink down. I closed my aching eyes and tried to shut off my train of thought about what could happen next.

� � �

It took two days before I got the first message on my phone from my father. I didn't even want to think about how he'd been able to find out my number.

Mark, you need to come back before your actions and health problems affect those closest to you.

Re-reading the message twice, the hand holding the phone shook even when I'd known deep down my father was never going to tolerate being threatened by anyone. It was short and to the point, and I debated with myself for several minutes before I got up and walked to the door to go down to the auto shop to talk to Sid.

Since he'd returned into the clubhouse minus the two goons who'd been given a little more incentive to not come back, Sid had been closed-lipped about everything except one thing, me staying in the apartment. He'd been very vocal about that when I'd waved my unbandaged hand under his nose.

I didn't have any reason now to stay with him. He had other ideas, ones I wanted to kick his ass for because I couldn't argue with them. Being alone left me vulnerable to attack. The auto shop had a security system that was state of the art, that my hand, though healed, was weak, and I'd struggle if I had to fight more than one attacker at a time. They were all reasonable, except for the one thing he'd failed to mention, him and me being alone together. There was nothing reasonable about my feelings for him or his avoidance of them. This left him exposed in my eyes. What if I revealed my feelings and someone noticed? My stomach knotted at the thought that anyone could use Sid against me.

It was getting harder every day to control how I felt, and I wasn't sure if Sid was just playing dumb to avoid what was going on, or he really couldn't see what was right in front of him. Shutting out the depressing feelings, I walked into the auto shop, my gaze sweeping around the busy space. The noise was so familiar that I hardly noticed the loud rock music or the clanging from tools hitting metal.

Sid was standing on the far side of the shop, his hands on his hips as he stared at the old Buick that looked ready for the scrap pile. Ram talked and pointed to something I couldn't see, but the look of disgust that came after left me chuckling.

As if Sid sensed me, his gaze shifted in my direction. I picked up my pace. "You got five?" I held up my phone, and Ram got a look of concern on his face.

"Is this club business?" he asked.

I didn't curse, though I wanted to. "I got a message from dear old dad."

Sid was already reaching for my phone, but I pulled my hand back. "You're covered in grease," I pointed out.

He scowled and rubbed his hands down the side of his overalls.

"I'll read it to you. *Mark, you need to come back before your actions and health problems affect those closest to you.*"

"That it?" The lines around Sid's mouth deepened.

"Yep, that's it. He was never one to waste words."

Sid glanced at Ram. "Go call Mason and see if he has some time to come here to talk."

I arched my brows. "Why Mason?"

"That's a threat, it might be veiled, but it's there in a message. Maybe Mason has some legal shit he can do. You never shared your number, so he's broken some law to get it. That's another strike against him. Mason's clever with the law. He'll know how to fight this part."

Sid sounded so sure of himself that I relaxed a little as I nodded. "Okay, we can play it that way."

"It's what we've got at the minute. Mason was clear, we fight the legal way...*first.*"

I laughed at the way Sid snapped out the last part like it tasted bad in his mouth. "I'll hang around down here until we hear something."

That got a nod from Sid. "What did the physical therapy dude say about using your hand?"

The change of topic threw me for a second. "I asked about workin', he said ten minutes every hour to either draw or work with the paints. And build up every two days by another five minutes." I shrugged, trying to hide my frustration at not being able to go straight back to work.

"Talkin' of drawings, did you ever do a sketch for my hog?"

The heat that crept up my neck was willed away as I met Sid's inquisitive stare. "Yep, it's in my cabinet." I nodded toward where my section was. "I's planned to show you the day I got injured."

His face broke into a massive, eager grin. "Go get it, let's have a look."

Fuck! I gritted my teeth as I swung around to do as he asked. At the sound of him following behind me, I didn't have any time to collect myself. Would he like what I'd done? I'd scrapped the drawings several times before I'd finally been happy with what I'd designed. His hog was something he treasured, and it was a big deal he'd asked me to create a design for it.

My hands were clammy as I pushed past the plastic sheeting to step into my workspace. I blew out a breath when the buzz started in my ears as I bent down to search through where I kept my designs. I could all but feel Sid's breath on the back of my neck, he was so close.

When I found what I was looking for, I slowly got up and faced Sid. Once more, I pulled my hand away as he went to take the drawing. "Nope, you ain't putting your grubby hands on it. It took me a fuckin' age to get it just the way I wanted it."

There was a look at his hands before he grumbled something I didn't quite catch under his breath while he stepped closer to me to peer over my shoulder. I held still as he looked down at what I'd poured my heart and soul into.

The serpent was coiled around the tank, and each scale had a tiny broken skull etched onto them. The snake was the same color as Sid's tattoo. The only difference was the eye color. I'd used Sid's, and they seemed to come right off the page with the 3D-effect I hoped to replicate on the tank. The fangs dripped with blood, but instead of droplets, there were words spelling out *Serpent*.

His breath touched my cheek as he moved, and I got a look at his face. My heart skipped several beats as he held my gaze. "It's...fuckin *beautiful*." His face became flushed.

An ache developed at the back of my eyes, and I blinked several times, fearful that I might actually cry at the depth of emotion Sid didn't appear to be able to hide. "I'm glad you like it," I croaked out.

"Like, nope, that doesn't even come close." I wasn't sure who was more shocked him or me as he closed the distance and kissed me. The wide eyes and heavy breathing were something we were both doing as he pulled back. "Fuck, you make me forget myself."

The frustration came off him in waves, and for a second, I thought he was going to say more, but then Ram appeared through the plastic wall, breaking the spell.

"Mason says he's got an hour this afternoon, but you have to go to his office."

Sid swore as I twisted to face Ram. "What time do I need to be there?"

"*We.* We need to be there," Sid added, his eyes firing all sorts of warning at me.

I rolled my eyes at both men. "What time do *we* need to be there?"

Chapter 19

SID

We opted to use the truck to drive to Killeen to go to Mason's office. Parking, I eyed Toad, who had been silent for the whole trip. "You okay?"

"I'm not sure what Mason can do, but if I continue to poke at the rattlesnake, at some point, the fucker is gonna bite and hard." The resignation was evident as he glanced at me, his shoulders slumped and deep grooves around his mouth.

"Let's forget the pessimism until after we've talked to Mason."

Toad gave me a whatever look, then got out of the cab. The Texas sun was baking, the thin T-shirt clung to my back as we walked side by side down the street to the large building where Mason's law practice was.

Toad eyed the building and sighed as he pushed open the door, favoring his right hand. The moment we walked into the entranceway, the woman at the desk in the reception area looked up, a smile on her lips. It didn't falter, and I gave her kudos for that.

"Can I help you, gentlemen?"

"We're here to see Mason," I answered.

"Mr. Davenport, is he expecting you?"

"Would we be here if he wasn't?" I ground out.

Toad laid a hand on my arm, his fingers digging in hard enough to keep me from saying more.

"Yes, Mr. Davenport is expecting us. We have an appointment for two pm." Toad gave the woman a polite smile.

"If you take a seat," she indicated to the row of chairs in muted gray next to the large glass window, "I'll advise his secretary you're here."

I grunted and headed for the seats. "Why don't they just tell us where to go?"

Toad chuckled. "Who knows."

We sat side by side, and I started to sweat as the sun baked the glass and me with it.

After three minutes of bitching, the woman appeared again, her smile polite as she ushered us to a lift. "Mr. Davenport is currently on a call. He'll meet us in the conference room." The secretary said as we exited the elevator into the hallway, where there was very little noise. The thick carpet cushioned the sound as we walked after the woman. I scratched at my neck, feeling more than a little out of my depth. I'd never been in a lawyer's office before. Toad, on the other hand, seemed comfortable as he appeared relaxed and unconcerned at the stuffiness of the place.

The woman stopped at the door, her smile still in place before she opened it. "Can I get either of you gentlemen a drink?"

"Water for me," Toad replied.

"Same," I tagged on, not sure I was going to be able to drink anything with how uncomfortable I was feeling.

The room had cream walls with pictures of snow scenes. A bookcase took up the whole of one wall and was filled with big leather-bound books. The table the secretary indicated for us to sit at was round and a dark wood. There were ten leather chairs in dark brown around it. Toad took one close to the large windows that gave you a view of Killeen's skyline. When the woman walked out, I moved over to the window to wound up to sit right then.

A second later, the door opened, and Mason appeared looking very much the lawyer in his suit and tie. I shook my head at the mystery of how someone like him and Linc could make it work.

"Thanks for comin' in, guys. I had back-to-back appointments, meaning I didn't have the time to come to the clubhouse." He gave us both a smile as he pulled out a seat and placed what he held on the table.

His secretary appeared with a tray with a jug of ice water and three glasses. "Do you need anything else, Mason?"

"No, we should be fine..." He waited till she left before he poured the water and offered it to us. "Okay, let's talk. What happened today, Toad?"

Toad pulled out his cell phone, unlocked the screen, and pressed a few buttons before pushing the cell phone to Mason. "I got a text from the old man. This number ain't registered to me. It's new after the two goons threw mine away. I mean I've only had it forty-eight hours."

Mason frowned as he read the message, picked up his pen, and started to scribble stuff on the pad he had in front of him. I walked to the table and sat next to Toad. To keep my hands occupied, I took hold of the glass. The condensation ran down the sides and wet my fingers as the chill distracted me.

"This isn't my area of law, but we'll figure it out. After the meeting at the clubhouse, I did a little research of my own."

"What, why?" Toad looked alarmed as he lurched forward in the chair he'd been relaxed in.

"I need to know what we're up against if I'm going to be able to help. Understanding what kind of clout your family has helps me."

"Helps you how?" I butted in, not liking how agitated Toad was becoming as his hand tapped nervously against the table.

"Firstly, to figure out where there are possible weaknesses that we can use to get Mr. Hanna to back off and leave Toad alone. Sending two guys to snatch him after not seeing his son for five years shows how committed he is to putting Toad back behind a locked door." He answered me, but his gaze never left Toad. "Do you have something on your father that he's frightened you'll use against him?"

"What do you mean? Besides lockin' his son in a mental institute and tellin' everyone I'm crazy, nope. He was never interested in sharing anything with me once he figured I was 'deformed' and 'unnatural.' His words, not mine." Pain was etched into his expression before he glanced away. "The old man is the worst kind of racist bigot. He also doesn't hide it either, so it's not like you can use that against him. His followers know what he's like."

The defeat was enough to tie me up in knots. "How the fuck do we fight that?" I growled, working on hiding my fear. Would Toad leave? Start a life somewhere else? The knots tightened when I didn't come up with an answer I liked.

"We fight using the law. It's there for a reason, and right now, your father has broken several of them. The number he's sent the message from, can you confirm that's his?" Mason tapped the pen on his lips as his eyes narrowed.

Toad nodded. "It is his. He's had the same one as long as he's had a cell phone. He's anal about things like that."

"That's good, so he can't deny that the message came from his cell phone. That allows us to question how he got your private number." Mason's lips pursed for several seconds as his expression turned thoughtful. "I'll talk to my father and see what we can come up with in regard to breaches in legislation. I'll then draw up an official letter to send on your behalf. You can read it, then I'll have it couriered. You're still stayin' with Sid?"

I wasn't sure this shit would work, but right then, it was all we had, so I clung to the hope it would keep Toad safe with the knowledge that Mason had worked his magic for Linc.

"I was planning on moving back to my apartment now that Sid doesn't need to take care of my hand," Toad answered without looking in my direction.

Floored for a second, I couldn't find a reply. When had he decided this?

Mason shook his head and threw a look of worry in my direction. "That's not a good idea. You need to be with someone at all times right now. They've tried once to take you with force. What's to say they won't try again? This message is a warning. After what you've told us about your family, I'd say they aren't messing around here."

As Mason pointed out the obvious, I started to relax until Toad stood and walked to the window, his body language shouting keep the fuck away.

"Maybe it's time to skip town and find somewhere else to live."

"You want to run for your whole life? That will eventually get old, then what? Hope your family will give up? I have a feeling you know already that's not going to happen." Mason got up and walked to Toad. "Listen to me, I don't know what it's like to live with fear, but I can't imagine it's great. Talk to Linc. He understands loss better than any of us. Please don't do anything rash right now. Give me a chance to help," he pleaded.

When Toad's shoulders sagged, I released the breath I'd been unaware I was holding. How was I going to stop Toad from leaving me?

That question turned into a pain in my ass as it replayed over and over as Toad returned to take a seat and listen to Mason talk through what he thought the options were. When we left an hour later, Toad looked sullen, and his face remained closed off.

As we exited the building, I grabbed his arm. "I'm hungry. Let's go grab something to eat."

That got a reaction. His eyes widened as he glanced about the busy street. "You wanna go somewhere public to eat...with me?"

I refused to shy away from the gleam he got in his eye. "Yep. Isn't that what I said?"

185

Since he'd come to see me to talk about the message, he hadn't been his usual cocky self, and until his confident smile returned, I didn't realize how much I missed it. "Just checkin'. Where did you have in mind?"

Shit! "No clue, I don't come here often."

The cell phone reappeared in his hand. "What you hungry for?" His eyes were on the phone as he tapped on the screen.

It was there right on the tip of my tongue to say you, but I kept that stupid shit to myself and answered, "Burger, with everything on it."

His fingers flew as his gaze remained on the small screen. "There's a place not far that has a good recommendation for burgers. Want to try it?"

"Whatever, as long as it's edible." Starting to feel really uncomfortable with how this was going, I poked his ribs with my elbow. "Come on, which way."

Ten minutes later, I was seated in a booth, the AC cooling my skin while my stomach growled at the heavenly scent of food.

The waitress handed us menus. Her name badge informed us her name was Mona. "What can I get you to drink?" Her smile was bright, and she didn't seem to notice or care what we looked like, not like the table of four guys to our left. They were paying us way more attention than I thought was necessary.

"I'll have a Coke, and so will he," Toad answered.

The waitress disappeared to get our drinks, saying she'd be back to take orders in a few minutes. The place was busy, and though it had a laidback feel, those around us mostly wore suits or army gear. This wasn't a surprise as Killeen had a big army base.

"You think they're on a date?" A guy at the table next to us asked loudly.

One of his buddies nudged him and shook his head as I glanced in their direction. I couldn't say what possessed me, but I reached over the table and took hold of Toad's hand, then looked at the four men. "Yep, you guessed it. But what the fuck business is it of yours?" I added an extra edge of mean to my reply, making sure they didn't miss that they were treading a dangerous line.

Chapter 20

TOAD

No way he'd said that. Did he? Convinced my head was on a spring, the way it moved between Sid and the four idiots asking for trouble. The guy who'd been stupid enough to voice the question paled as Sid continued to give him what I'd have called *his shut up or die* stare.

"We don't want no trouble in here," Mona said as she reappeared, wearing an exasperated expression as she eyed the four men before focusing on us.

"It's all good. We'll have the house special with two large sides of fries and slaw." Sid didn't contradict me. He remained staring at the guys.

The tension increased as the waitress wrote down what I'd ordered.

"Apologize to my date for bein' rude."

My heart thrummed faster than a hummingbird's wings as the guy's Adam's apple repeatedly bobbed at the anger Sid was directing at him.

Shifting to make sure I could get out of the booth and dive in if this headed south, I kept my gaze on Sid.

"Sorry," the guy mumbled.

At that point, Sid dismissed the table and turned his attention back to me. "What did you order...hon?"

I choked as I tried to swallow back the laughter. My lips quivered as I kept my gaze on Sid. I'd never seen this side of him, and if I'd already not fallen hard for his ass, this would have tipped me over the edge. "The house special...darlin'."

Humor lit up his eyes as he nodded and relaxed back against the leather, flexing his bicep as his arm draped over the back of the seat.

About two minutes later, the table next to us cleared out. It was only after they left that I let go of the laughter. "You're a funny man."

A smile he didn't often display spread over his face. "Can be when it's called for."

I chuckled. "And you think threatenin' folks is when it's called for?"

"They were bein' dicks. And it's a," he squirmed on the seat before looking directly at me, "date, right?"

The humor of the situation left faster than a getaway car as I lurched forward in my seat, unable to contain my reaction. "Say what?"

Dark color flooded his face. "You heard, stop bein' a prick. It's what you want, ain't it?"

The anger mixed with uncertainty stopped me from snapping back that I didn't need his pity. "Why now? Is this just to stop me leavin'?" I held my breath as he appeared to contemplate his answer.

"In part—"

"Then forget it—"

"Fuck's sake, let me finish," he growled as the waitress returned with the food, stopping the conversation.

Once the food was on the table, Sid ran a hand over his bald head and eyed me with what looked like trepidation. "I told you in the beginnin' that I don't do relationships, fuckin is what I do with no repeats." He licked his lips, then picked up his drink and drank deep before continuing, "You're different. Fuck if I can get you out of my head. When those fuckers took you..." he glanced away, but not before I could see gut-wrenching fear. When he looked back, it was gone. "I don't have flowery words or any shit like that. I like you a lot. Can we leave it at that?"

"Not quite. Are we doin' this?" I pointed between us. "Are you gonna tell the brothers we're... together."

He looked more resigned than upset as his head slowly moved to confirm he would. Was he doing this just to keep me here? The question was a bitch and wasn't ready to stop nagging at me. "Are you sure this is about more than what's goin' on in my life right now?"

"Jeez, can't you just fuckin' accept what I said? What's happenin' made me see things differently. I don't want you to leave...me." His frustration was evident in every word.

The scowl aimed at me was murderous when he finished, but I didn't give a shit, not when my heart was so fucking full. "Cool." I picked up my burger and took a big mouthful, suddenly feeling ravenous.

He shook his head but followed suit.

The meal was demolished quickly, and we were heading back to Belton in the evening traffic. The asphalt had a haze across its surface as the sun was merciless. Sweat—I wasn't sure if it was due to the heat or what could possibly happen when we got back to the apartment—beaded on my skin.

Sid remained silent for the journey back and only spoke when we hit the edge of town. "Clubhouse...or the apartment?"

His gaze remained on the windshield, his face an unreadable mask. "Apartment." The only acknowledgment I received was that he indicated at the next junction to head toward the auto shop. My pulse skipped several beats, and I got air stuck in the back of my throat at the thought of what was going to happen when we got back to the apartment. I didn't fool myself about what I wanted to happen. Sid under me, on me, around me, in me, anyway I could get him. I'd thought about little else since the first time. I balled my hands to keep the shaking from becoming obvious as he parked.

The parking lot was empty because it was after six. We both sat for a moment, neither saying anything, then I reached for the door. Silently, he followed suit. We exited the cab together and walked side by side to the door that led up to his home.

I pressed against his back, enjoying the shudders running through him as he unlocked the main door. "I'm going to give you everything you want," I whispered.

"We'll see," he answered in a strained tone.

I chuckled and pushed a little harder against him, making sure he felt my arousal. "Is that so. Are you sayin' you don't want me to shove you over the first flat surface and...fill you till you can't think about anything other than my cock?"

This time he pressed back against me, his chest rising and falling rapidly. The keys hung in the lock, apparently forgotten. "You teasin' fucker." He groaned as my hand came round his hip and moved to slide over the front of the hard bulge in his jeans.

"You think I'm teasin' you? Last time you only let me fuck you, this time I'm going to take you apart with my mouth, tongue, fingers, and only when you beg will I fuck you the way you want." I ground hard against him as I bit his ear. "Hard and fast, darlin'."

I was practically holding all his weight as he pushed back impatiently, trying to get me closer to him. My rumble of laugher got another groan as my body moved against his. "Open the door, now?" I demanded in a deep, authoritative voice I knew he loved.

It took a second before he managed to get the door open and moving, his reluctance to move away from me doing all sorts of crazy shit to my cock. I let him have enough room to get up the stairs, but that was it.

Once we were inside the apartment, Sid didn't turn to face me, and I smiled as I came up behind him, taking hold of his large body. One hand holding his throat, the other his hip. I settled his head on my shoulder, his large body pressed against me. "I want you to strip for me." I kissed my way from the side of his face down his neck, where I bit gently on the bristly skin.

"Then let go?" he rasped.

I did, slowly and easily stepping back so he could turn. His face was flushed, pupils consumed his eyes, making them appear black as his trembling hands dragged off his T-shirt. The remaining clothes followed until he was standing, aroused and visibly shaking.

His gaze moved down my body. "You gonna strip?"

"When you're beggin' for more."

His nostrils flared, and a look of defiance appeared as his chin jutted out, yet he didn't dispute what I'd said. "Your bedroom, now."

I didn't wait to see what he'd do as I walked past him doing my best to steady my breathing. I wanted to do this right. The first time I'd been so caught up in the moment that I hadn't given Sid's body the attention it warranted. It was a thing of beauty. Hard muscles, covered in smooth skin that showed some of the battle scars he'd earned as a brother in Dark Angels. The tattoos added to the overall appeal and showed off his true nature.

I stopped at the side of his unmade, large bed. "Supplies?"

"Top drawer," he pointed to the wooden chest against the far wall, "over there."

There was a hint of nervousness that, if memory served me right, hadn't been there the first time we'd been together. This was different for both of us.

As that settled inside me, it took off the edge of desperation I felt as I went to retrieve the lube and condoms. He remained standing by the bed, unmoving as he watched me place what I'd found on the bed.

The tension between us grew and the air crackled with the energy of it. "Lay down on your front."

Without hesitation, he did as I asked, his head resting on a pillow he pulled toward him and wrapped his arms around. It was as if he understood he would need something to hold on to, and I swallowed the chuckle at how right he was.

I tapped his left leg. "Open for me, darlin'." He shivered as he did, spreading his legs wide enough for me to kneel between them. One knee on the bed, I cursed my clothing and the promise I'd given him. I shook my head, glad he couldn't see me struggling before I knelt between his thighs after taking off my boots.

His ass flexed, but I didn't have any intention of going there...yet. I shifted over him and caged him in, placing my arms on either side of his head, holding my body away from his. He made a sound in the back of his throat as I pressed a kiss between his shoulder blades. This was followed by my tongue licking the warm flesh. Another shudder proceeded a whimper as my lips trailed down his back: kiss, lick, shudder. It set a pattern until I reached his lower back.

There were only the sounds he made as I continued to explore each dip of his buttocks with my mouth. The two indents at the top of his buttocks got a curse, and I chuckled. On and on, I explored his body, measuring his reaction to each kiss each caress. Paying extra attention to the places that got him a bigger reaction. By the time

I'd worked down his thighs, he was slowly humping at the cover beneath him.

My heart felt full as I moved back up and whispered close to his ear, "You ready to beg yet?"

Chapter 21

SID

Beg, I couldn't even fucking remember my own name, never mind form a sentence that would make any sense. I grunted into the pillow and lifted my ass, hoping he'd get the fucking hint and give me what I wanted.

His hand smacked hard on my ass, and I jerked up, the sting warming more than my cheeks. My cock pulsed against the cover beneath me as I glared over my shoulder. "I ain't a child who needs a spanking."

His eyes gleamed, and that was the only warning I got. The next two hard smacks to my ass left me confused by the flood of precum that dampened the sheet. My ass burned, causing the need to come to push to the forefront. What had been arousing but mellow switched to something that wasn't as easily controlled.

"I know you ain't a child." His hand went between my legs, and his fingers firmly tugged on my balls, the ache adding to the torment. "But a little pain can add somethin'," his voice dropped several octaves as his eyelids lowered a fraction, "extra. Don't think." To make his point, the hand holding my balls squeezed as he spanked the other ass cheek hard enough that it left my backside throbbing.

"Motherfucker!" I cried out. My body's reaction giving me away.

The chuckle was dark and dangerous as his breath touched my hot ass a second before his teeth sank into the hot flesh. His hand released my balls, but I didn't get a chance to breathe easily as his hand took hold of the root of my cock and tugged it down between my legs. The teeth released and a warm, wet tongue licked at the tender spot. His fingers slid over the head of my cock, using my precum as slick. His fingernail dug into the head of my cock, distracting me from where his mouth was headed. The second his tongue reached my hole, I clenched. The feelings were nothing like I'd ever experienced before. I couldn't keep my mouth shut. "Arghhhh...whattt...oh...fuck!" I couldn't keep still as I pushed up and back, wanting more of his mouth as he chose then to move away.

"So needy. You ready to beg?"

He sounded as wired as I felt as I buried my head in the pillow and he continued to tease the slit of my cock, leaving my ass untouched. I wanted him to touch me so fucking bad right then I'd have given him whatever he wanted. Over the years, I'd never let anyone touch me in this way. The shame I'd felt ensured I'd been the one doing the fucking, hiding my own needs. The very first time with Toad, he'd somehow understood what I craved without me saying a word. He'd rocked my world, and I should have known then that I had feelings for him. That I'd never be able to keep my distance.

The hand disappearing from my body got me out of my head as I growled without thought, "Don't stop, fuck, you know what I want."

The T-shirt he wore stopped me from feeling his skin against mine as he pressed his chest against me. His erection felt hard and hot through his jeans next to my ass cheek. "What is it you want?" His lips pressed to my jaw. "Tell me, and I'll give it to you," he promised in a sultry voice that would have tempted the fucking devil himself.

I sucked in a shaky breath and willed the words out of my mouth, knowing the bastard wouldn't give me what I want unless I asked—begged. "Do all the things you promised. I want all of it. I'm beggin' so just get fuckin' on with it."

My impatience got a wicked smile before he pressed one more kiss to the edge of my lips. "As you asked so nicely." His sarcasm was lost under the humor as he got off me, and I twisted my head to watch him strip. Confidence that was a real turn-on exuded off him as he didn't waste time taking off his clothes. I swallowed the sigh of relief when he finally got back on the bed, having gloved his cock.

But the fucker didn't do as I expected. Instead he got me to roll over and started back with the kissing and licking he'd been doing, only this time down the front of my body. The tension coiled tight, and his tempting mouth and fingers plucked at my control like he was playing a tune on fucking guitar. Yet, deep down, I never wanted it to end. In my whole life, I'd never felt so *treasured*. He paid homage to me in ways that my heart understood and my soul had craved, but I had ignored.

The reverence with which he touched me as his fingers sank into my body, preparing me for what was coming, left me speechless. I gasped as he caressed my prostate, his gaze never leaving mine. "Say your mine," he ground out through his bunched jaw.

The intensity of his stare increased until all I could see and feel was him. "I am," I whispered back, feeling way too vulnerable. My eyelids dropped to shield my emotions as I worked to catch my breath.

"Don't hide from me," he begged with all the emotion I was feeling. "See me, know me, I…" he paused and licked at his lips.

Heart hammering against my ribs, I couldn't catch my breath, understanding that this moment was going to change things between us. The words might be hard for him to say, but his eyes had none of the same issues. The love was there, and for once, I understood what it was like to have someone care enough to show me that level of affection. Precum cooled on my skin as his hand stilled, and we stared at each other intently.

"The bar you go to for a hookup was the first time I saw you." I frowned, trying to decipher where this was leading. "That was before I followed you to Belton and applied to be a prospect with Dark Angels."

A buzz started out low in my ears as I struggled to sit up and digest what he was saying. I didn't get far as he carefully removed his fingers from my ass and his other hand pushed on my shoulder. Then he pressed me into the mattress, his cock nestling next to mine, attempting to distract me. "I'm not followin'."

"You are the reason I moved to Belton. The moment I set eyes on you, I wanted you. The feelings I have for you have been growing from that moment. I know you have a way to catch up with me." His directness increased the buzzing in my ears to deafening.

"I—"

His lips pressed to mine, stopping me from saying anything more. His tongue ran along the seam of my lips, demanding entry. Lost against the need he evoked in me, I gave in. The taste of him left me wanting more. His hands moved down the sides of my body and under my ass. His hips lifted, and his cock pressed against my hole. The pressure light to start with as he deepened the kiss. His tongue swirled around mine before he sucked mine into his mouth just as he pushed his cock past the tight ring of muscle. The burn would have been breathtaking if Toad had given me a chance to breathe. His mouth commanded mine as his cock pushed in inch by inch until I couldn't think, only feel. The fullness of the stretch everything I remembered, and it left me questioning why I hadn't given in sooner.

His pelvis met mine, chest heaving, his mouth moved to kiss a path down my jaw until his lips reached my ear. "I love you," he whispered as he withdrew then pushed back in hard. The confession, along with the powerful, deep strokes, left me too close to the edge. Whirling emotions flooded through me, taking me to the point of no return way too fucking fast.

Struggling to think about anything other than the man above me, taking me apart piece by piece, my teeth clenched in an attempt to take back control. As if he sensed what I was trying to do, his mouth claimed mine once more as the speed of his thrusts increased. Sounds of flesh hitting flesh were followed by the heavy scent of sex as Toad did as he'd promised, and I lost the battle. Cum spread between us as I gasped into his mouth. He didn't stop, his kisses driving me higher until my cock gave its last-ditch attempt to give Toad what he wanted. Heat filled my ass, and Toad's lips left mine to roar his pleasure, head tilting back his eyes scrunched tightly shut, the whole while his body shuddered violently.

When he collapsed against my sweat and cum-drenched body, his hot breath came in short bursts over my neck.

"That was—"

"Mind-blowing," he finished. "Gimme five, then let's see if we can top it."

I chuckled for the first time in my life after sex. "Maybe give me ten," I joked back, my eyes drifting shut as he kissed the pulse beating in my neck.

Chapter 22

Sid was doing his best to pretend we hadn't had a moment together, that I hadn't declared my feelings. But I wasn't letting him get away with it. He sat next to Linc in church as Linc went through what he wanted from the brothers in terms of protection for me.

Unfortunately, dear old dad wasn't happy with the legal letter Mason had sent. The sheriff's men had come to the club hours earlier to hassle the club brothers while they were minding their own business. They'd come up with some bullshit about reports of complaints about fighting, this, it appeared, required them to check out every fucking room in the clubhouse. Tina had rung Linc, who'd called Mason, which had been the end of the search.

Only it hadn't ended there because Linc had left the tattoo shop to come to the club and gone toe to toe with the dick of a sheriff. Eventually, Mason had got it all smoothed out, but as the dick had left, he'd all but promised he'd be back. It was too much of a coincidence that it was happening now. It left a bad taste in my mouth that this was, without a doubt, connected to me. Linc seemed to think the same and why we were back in church to talk about this shit, again.

Mason was becoming a permanent feature at these meetings. It showed exactly how much Linc trusted him. Had the other brothers noticed?

"Toad's father is a powerful man, and as Toad pointed out, he has a lot of political reach and friends. My law firm has had a firm based in D.C. contact us to advise it would be in our best interests not to represent Toad." Anger Mason didn't try to hide left me with a surge of panic.

"See, this is the shit I didn't want touchin' you or anyone—"

Linc's gaze landed on me, and I shut up at the warning flashing in his eyes. "This is club business. We'll deal with whatever comes our way...*together*. You became a member understanding that brothers fight as one."

I nodded, feeling chastised as Sid started to shift in his seat. "Sorry, I do. I just hate what's happenin' right now. This is only the beginnin'."

"That might be so, but your father is making assumptions about what happens here," Mason said as he lifted up a file that had been on the table. "The visit from the sheriff today proved that. Your father is assuming that Dark Angels members aren't law-abiding citizens." That got a round of laughter; even Linc's lips twitched. "Today, they went away with their tail firmly tucked between their legs. I'm sure you're right that this is only the beginning. The sheriff has too much history with Dark Angels not to want to listen to some trumped-up crap he's being fed. Our defense is to fight fire with fire. What your father seems to have forgotten is that gathering information, that's current, on those you chose to fight is essential when going into battle. It's sloppy and stupid not to do that." A flinty gleam appeared in Mason's eyes. "His arrogance will be his downfall."

There was something in the way Mason spoke that spiked my pulse as the file he'd picked up was opened. A dark smile spread over his face, one that Linc would struggle to rival. "In here, I have information that pertains to some of your father's not-so-secret deals. This information in the wrong hands could do untold damage to his political aspirations. Aspirations he's made no secret of. After I'd spoken to all the lawyers in our firm. None of whom like to be threatened, it was agreed we'll deal with this case. I have a crack team that loves nothing more than digging into other people's lives. It was easy to find some...*dirt*." He chuckled.

Linc gave Mason a grin that he rarely offered anyone else. Sid glanced in my direction, his own smile similar to Linc's, and my breath caught in my throat. Everyone else in the room disappeared as I stared back at Sid. The seconds stretched, with my heart hoping that the feelings he kept on a tight leash were really what I saw and not just my imagination.

"—that will be the next step," Mason finished, looking expectantly at me.

"Fuck, sorry I...missed that last part." I refused to let my discomfort show as I turned my attention to Mason.

Mason's lips quivered, a light dancing in his eyes as he closed the file. "I'll be taking a trip to D.C. to meet with your father to lay out the terms of him backing off, *forever*."

"I'll come with you." It was out before I could think better of it.

Sid was out of his seat a split second later. "The fuck you will."

The room went deadly quiet as Linc looked between the pair of us, his eyes narrowing.

"You don't get to decide," I gritted out.

Sid's features set into a look I recognized, stubbornness. "Aren't we together? Ain't that what you said?" He pointed between us. "Aren't couples supposed to make these decisions *together*?" He couldn't have been any clearer about what was happening between us.

There were several gasps from those around us. I didn't take my eyes off Sid. He'd said he'd let the brothers know about us, but I hadn't quite expected…this. And if I wasn't mistaken, I'd say neither had he by the strained expression. "Is this the place you wanna talk about this?" I asked, making sure to bring Sid's attention to the other men in the room.

"I don't give a fuck where we discuss it, you ain't goin' to D.C." His whole body appeared to be readying for attack the way he stood poised above me.

Understanding the chain of command in Dark Angels didn't mean the same in my relationship with this stubborn fool, I wasn't going to let him tell me what I could and couldn't do. However, choosing to have that discussion in front of the brothers was not something I would do. "We'll talk about it *later.*"

Mason got up and stood between us. "I get your concerns, Sid, I do." He looked directly at Sid as he spoke, meaning I couldn't see his expression. "So I suggest you come too." Mason glanced about the room, and he got a thoughtful expression. "Maybe you all should come. A show in strength can't hurt."

Linc got up, his hand running through his hair. "It would need to be planned, so folks can get time off." His gaze moved to the club members who'd remained silent throughout the exchange. "Who'd be up for a road trip to D.C.? The club would fund the expenses."

There was a roar of approval as Mason shook his head. "Do you need to be so loud?"

Things got louder as shouts turned to raucous laughter before everyone settled down. Sid didn't look at me as he returned to his seat, and I got the sinking feeling that we'd be having our first official fight when we got back to the apartment. I swallowed a sigh, masking my thoughts as I listened to what was going to happen next.

💀 💀 💀

Sid hadn't done the predictable. Instead he'd stalked off after the meeting, leaving me to make my own way back to the apartment. That had been ten hours ago, and he still hadn't returned. Had he gone to fuck some stranger to prove he didn't...

I shut my thoughts down, having already spent hours worrying about what Sid was up to or where he was. After I'd paced half the night, I'd given up and tried to sleep. That had been equally as useless with the scent of sex on the sheets as I'd opted to sleep in Sid's bed.

The sun was barely up when I showered and dressed to head down to the auto shop. With the need to do something to distract me, I chose work. Painting was where I could lose myself. It had been something I'd done often when I was younger. The talent was never nurtured by my folks, who thought it was a waste of my time. The aspiration of going to art school had never materialized. Instead I'd found ways in which I could use my love and talent.

Downstairs, I stopped at the back of the open workshop. The lights were blazing, and the sound of heavy rock was pouring out of the speakers mounted high on walls so the sound could be heard over everyday noise. Had Sid come here last night? I walked silently through the shop, searching for the man in question. Coming up empty, I headed to the small office that was at the back of the shop. The door was open a crack, so I peered through before a smile slid over my face at the sight of Sid fast asleep, slouched in the chair, looking more than a little uncomfortable in the cramped seat. His head was dipped and his chin rested on the top of his chest. He was filthy, showing he'd been working before he'd come in the office.

I couldn't see his face fully, but I didn't need to. I'd memorized it. Every line, mark, and crease, every expression he had, they were all there inside my head. The strain of wondering if he'd gone off and done something rash disappeared with the reality that Sid wasn't the kind of person to hurt someone intentionally unless they crossed him. The walls that protected his heart were understandable, but I wanted him to let me in desperately. Isn't that what he did at the clubhouse in front of everyone he classed as family? Rubbing a hand over my jaw, I stood for another minute, looking my fill as I ran through what had happened the day before.

Was he now regretting what he'd done?

With no answer, I left him sleeping. Shutting the door gently behind me, I walked over to my work area, needing something to distract me from the self-doubt. Razor had brought back his bike, and I'd started slowly finishing the other side of the tank. I put on a pair of overalls and put a glove over the nearly fully healed hand. The scarred skin wasn't as tight as I'd thought it was going to be after the damage the paint had caused. Sid had made sure the paints with the same ingredients were removed from the shop. Only one more thing to add to the list of things he'd done for me. If I were honest, I missed the care he lavished on me. He'd spent way more time than the nurses had using the ointments and oils the hospital had given me.

I flexed my fingers, and although they were still weaker than I'd have liked, I thanked whoever was up there that I still had use of them. Part of that was Sid helping—caring for—me.

Inhaling the scent of grease and paint, I shut my eyes for a moment and let the feelings that were always there when I thought of Sid to settle before releasing the breath.

It's gonna be okay.

Chapter 23

SID

There was a sort of tense truce between Toad and me after I'd fallen asleep last week in the shop. He hadn't said a word about it when I'd finally woken, stiff and sore to find him working on Razor's bike. I'd grunted as I'd gone past to go shower and get cleaned up, which had only gotten me a look I couldn't decipher. Since then, we'd been circling each other, not bringing up the issue of going to D.C. Not that anyone but me saw it as a problem. When I'd gone to the tattoo shop the next day, Linc had shut me down hard and fast. Instead he'd done something I hadn't expected and had sat me down to give me relationship advice.

"Sit and listen because I hate doin' this shit." *Linc pointed to the seat he used when tattooing.*

I grunted and took the seat. "He don't need to go to fuckin' D.C."

"Stop this bullshit. Toad wants to face his past, and that takes balls. Don't make this about you."

Up off the chair, I bumped chests with Linc. "What's that supposed to mean?" I bit out angrily.

He pushed me back hard enough that I rocked on the heels of my boots. "You ain't usin' me to get rid of your frustration. Now sit the fuck down." His eyes were firing warning shots any fool would be stupid not to step back from.

I sucked in a deep breath in the hope that it would help take the edge off the fear that wouldn't let me settle since I'd walked away from Toad the night before. "Sorry," I muttered, finally sitting back down.

"What I mean is that you're leadin' with your heart, not your head. Love changes shit." He rubbed at his jaw, his expression masking his thoughts. "The brothers will have his back. And Mason has the legal crap covered. So stop actin' like a prick."

I jerked at the sound of Ram's voice. "Fuck, you're a genius." Ram wiped a filthy hand over his overalls, his gaze still on the engine I'd barely finished fixing.

Pulling my thoughts to back what I'd been doing, I stared at the engine housing that had been an utter bitch to fix. "I hate to be fuckin' beat."

Ram flashed me a grin. "You're gonna make Miss Withers one happy lady. That engine should

216

have been condemned, and now she purrs like a fuckin' kitten."

"Dude, it works. That's all that matters." I nodded at the panel work that still needed doing. "The rest is up to you and Dex."

Ram sighed as his gaze moved over the rust bucket. "Yeah, we're gonna start on that this afternoon. There wasn't any point startin' till the engine was sorted."

I slapped him on the shoulder, leaving a grease stain behind. "She's all yours now."

The crestfallen expression got a laugh from me as the light of eagerness in his eyes couldn't quite be concealed at getting a chance to restore the old car.

Leaving him to it, I went over to Toad's workspace and lifted the plastic when I saw him in the corner, seated on a rickety chair, hunched over. The jeans and a T-shirt showed he hadn't been working on Razor's bike, which was in the closed-off area he used for spray painting. There was a pad on his knees, his focus fully fixed on what he was doing. He lifted up his right hand, still holding a pencil as he rubbed at the back where the skin was puckered. "It botherin' you?"

He glanced up, his eyes not quite focused before he blinked, then nodded. "It cramps, but it's better than it was." He shrugged as his gaze swept up and down my body.

My cock liked the attention it had been denied this last week. Toad had made a point of sleeping

217

in his own bed since the night I'd stayed up working, and I wasn't sure if it was because of the argument or if something else was bothering him.

Stop being a cocksucker and ask him what's up.

"You need to stop then. Give yourself a break," I said instead.

"It'll pass." He glanced back at the pad, dismissing me.

The frustration of the last week surfaced, and I stomped across the room to snatch the pencil from his grip. "Stop—"

"I'm workin'," he snapped back, his eyes firing all sorts of warnings that did little to cool my own temper or desire.

"You're hurtin' yourself," I fired back, pointing to his hand, "by doin' too much."

He stood in a measured way to place the pad on the counter next to him. Only then did he look me in the eye. "You wanna fight?" He stepped close enough to press his body against mine. "Or do you wanna fuck?"

The latter was said in a deep guttural tone that left me hard and aching. The fucker knew it too as he dared me with those tempting eyes of his. My hands fisted at my sides before I swung around and said in a controlled voice, "Apartment, now."

I didn't wait to see if he'd follow as I marched out the door and around the side of the building. The sound of footfalls behind me allowed me to release a breath and take another as I mounted the stairs to open the apartment door.

No sooner had I walked through the door, Toad behind me, than the door slammed shut. "I've warned you, I don't take to bein' ordered around."

The distance between us disappeared as I pushed my chest against his, knocking him back against the door. "I'm fuckin' worried about you." The bite of anger was sharp enough to draw blood as he glared back at me.

He flipped me fast and pushed my chest to the wall with a hard thud, his chest pressed to my back and the scent of paint and grease surrounding us. His mouth fastened on the side of my neck as one hand traveled down the side of my overalls. Those magic fingers undid the zipper and slipped in like a guided missile to my fly. Seconds later, his hand was inside my underwear. Before I could take a much-needed breath, he pumped my shaft hard and fast. The calloused, dry palm added friction and got me close to the edge of losing my load way too fast.

"This what you want, my hands on you?" he rasped in my ear before his tongue licked down the side of my throat. His teeth grazing over the sensitive skin at the junction of my neck.

"Yes," I growled. What was the point in denying it? I wanted whatever this man would give me.

His teeth sunk into the flesh just above the collar of my overalls, and he bit hard enough for my cock to reveal how much it wanted what was happening. "You want me to make you come like this? Or do you want me to fuck you right here where we're standin'?"

Breathless, the air wheezed past my lips. "Anything."

The speed of his hand increased, and my legs buckled while he ground his solid cock against my ass. His other hand slid under the edge of my T-shirt and moved up my chest. Nimble fingers took hold of a nipple and twisted it hard enough to bring tears to my eyes. I cried out as he dug a nail into the slit of my cock at the same time. Sensation overload, I wheezed like an asthmatic when hot cum spurted over the hand that continued to pump my cock, not slowing the pace as he milked me dry.

Before I could recover, Toad rasped, "Now get on your knees and suck me dry." I was released so fast my head spun. I turned on my shaky legs to see Toad licking the cum off his hand. A sexy smirk on his face, he looked at the floor and the empty space between his legs, brows lifting.

It was embarrassing how fast I moved, but I couldn't give a rat's ass when this was about pleasuring the man who'd turned my world upside down since he'd stepped into my life. Opening the front zip of his jeans, I teased him, taking my time to run my fingers over the bulge in the front of his underwear. The guttural groan spurred me on as my mouth watered for what was going to happen next.

The wicked glint that appeared in his eyes as he watched me made it hard to swallow. "You know I'll only make you pay for teasin' me, don't cha?"

I shuddered at the dark promise. Releasing his cock, I leaned forward and swallowed him down to the root. The scent and taste of him making my cock twitch with life. His hands slid around the back of my head, his eyes on me the whole time. I relaxed my throat, knowing what was going to happen next. Saliva dripped off my chin as I struggled to swallow around the thick length filling my mouth.

Excitement buzzed through me at the look of approval as his grip tightened and he took control. Each thrust, groan, and grunt was like a caress to my dick. His gaze never wavered from mine as he held me captive, controlling what was happening between us. This was what I'd craved secretly, being taken. Being allowed to let go in the moment, not thinking about anything, but left to just feel. How Toad understood that, I wasn't sure, and I didn't try to.

His shaft thickened, and I swallowed, clasping the head of his cock with my throat, causing him to moan loudly. Breaking eye contact first, he threw his head back, and cum slid down my throat along with my own strangled groan. I shifted a little back, eager to taste him.

"Fuck," he muttered as he pulled out of my mouth, his hands dropping to his sides. My dick throbbed as he stared down at me. "So fucking hard for me." Down on his knees, he kissed my mouth hard, his tongue dueling with mine. The lingering taste of my own cum mixed with his.

"Please, suck me," I begged against his mouth.

He released my mouth and grinned. "Stand up."

I didn't need to be asked twice. Standing, I wrapped my hand around my dick and held it out toward the other man. There were no words as his lips wrapped around me, and he sucked me deep into his mouth. A hand took hold of my balls and gave them a squeeze as his tongue swirled over the head of my dick. Then his cheeks hollowed as he sucked hard enough to make my eyes slam shut and a squeal I'd never admit to pass my lips. It was fast and dirty as he sucked, slurped, and fingered my ass until I shot my load down his throat not even two minutes later.

He sat back and ran his hand over his wet lips. "You wanna talk now?"

I swallowed the moan of complaint with the sex high still making me feel mellow and not in the mood to talk. "Why the cold shoulder?"

Moving slowly, he got up off the ground, adjusting his clothes. I did the same, suddenly feeling uncertain. Once his cock was back in his pants, he walked over to the couch, sitting. He tapped at the cushion next to him.

"It wasn't the cold shoulder," he started to explain as I sat down. "I was givin' you space to sort your head out." He took hold of my hand and twisted on the cushion to face me. "You disappeared on me. When I found you downstairs in the shop, that said you needed space." I went to interrupt, and he shook his head. "Let me finish. I get that this," he pointed between us, "is hard for you. I'm tryin' to do what's best for you, for me, and for the brothers. D.C. needs to happen. I have to face the past. I can't have a life here with you and keep havin' to look over my shoulder. Love changes things. You can be used against me. I'll never forgive myself if that happens."

The seriousness of his expression was combined with so much love; it did funny things to me. I'd swear it was that as I blurted out, "I think I love you."

He laughed, a rich, bold sound as his hand squeezed mine hard. "You're killin' me, dude, with the 'think.'"

"What's fuckin' funny?" I gritted out, feeling more than a little uncomfortable right then.

He tugged me toward him, but I resisted until he tutted and yanked hard enough that I overbalanced and landed half on him, our hands trapped between us. "You. You're funny, but I'm laughin' with you, not at you, dick. I love you, and it fuckin' fills me up hearin' you say it back. Even with the 'think.'" He pressed his forehead to mine, his eyes conveying the truth of his words.

"I never wanted this," I growled. "But I wouldn't change any of it. Not one damn thing." I claimed his mouth before he could say another word and let myself believe, if only for a moment, that life wasn't a shit storm always wanting to take something from me.

Chapter 24

TOAD

Mason paced in front of me, Linc, and Sid as he talked through what had now been arranged for the trip to D.C. in two days. I hadn't received any more word from dear old dad, but that meant jack shit. The sheriff had been on the prowl around the auto shop and the tattoo shop, but he'd done nothing more than let us know he was watching.

"After calculating how long it would take to get to D.C., we're flying."

"You mean after you realized you'd be on the back of my hog for hours and hours," Linc chimed in, looking more than a little amused.

"Fuck off," Mason said without breaking pace. "The flights are booked, along with the hotel closest to the address you gave us, Toad."

I nodded, chuckling. "That should give the good old folks of downtown Washington something to talk about."

Deep lines appeared around Mason's mouth. "Yeah, well. Let's hope it doesn't generate too much talk until after we've visited your father."

"He'll be aware we're there before we've exited the plane. So I wouldn't worry about that." Sid's hand moved to cover mine, and I turned my hand over and intertwined our fingers. My heart gave a little leap as it did every time Sid showed his affection without worrying about what anyone else thought. Over the last couple of weeks, it had been a gradual thing. The kiss he'd given me in front of the brothers in the clubhouse had been… a stamp of possession? To say he was in a relationship with me was one thing, but to openly show affection, yeah, that had been a real shocker.

"Is that going to be a problem?" Linc's question drew me from my thoughts.

"It'll be what it will be. The old man is predictable in that he's not predictable." I shrugged off my own nervousness. It was too late now to have an anxiety attack over what was going to go down. I'd meant what I'd said to Sid, I had to face this head-on, or I'd spend the rest of my life worrying about Sid.

The feelings I had for him, they'd changed everything. No matter how much I hated the thought of facing my family, the idea of losing Sid was worse. So I would suck it up and pray that

Mason's fat file of incrementing evidence, along with Dark Angels, would protect us from future attacks.

"Are you worried?" Linc questioned from his relaxed position in one of the leather chairs where he'd sat when he'd entered the clubhouse half-an-hour ago.

It was a hard question to answer because there was no simple answer when it involved my heart. "I'm concerned about them figuring out I love Sid."

The man seated next to me stiffened, then his fingers tightened painfully around mine. "You think they'll go after me?"

His voice gave nothing away, and neither did his expression as I looked at him. "Yeah, I do. They attack any weak spot. For me, that's you." I breathed out a shaky breath at laying out the fear.

Linc got up and stood just in front of Sid and me. Mason followed and wrapped his arm around Linc's waist. "We've got your backs." Linc looked around the room. Men and women stood and came over, forming a circle around Sid and me.

I lost the feeling in my fingers, but I didn't complain as Sid got a look of pride on his face. "We'll show them you don't fuck with us."

Any remaining worry I'd been unable to shake disappeared as I met Sid's determined stare. "Okay, we got this."

The flight was uneventful if I ignored the stares of people as we got on and off the plane. Twenty-three men and women dressed as we were, wearing our leather patches to identify who we were. Yeah, there was nothing subtle about us. The only person missing was Nutty, who'd stayed behind with River. Linc had reached out to Dog and Rattlesnake from the Chosen Few club, who were only too happy to do Linc a favor for one in return, though that was as yet to be determined. They'd sent three of their club members to come and protect River while we were away.

It was all part of the plan Mason had concocted, so no one was left vulnerable. The man had some smarts, as did the team he worked with. I hadn't been aware of half the crap the old man had been involved in. Mason had enough shit to bury my father up to his stiff neck. The game of cat and mouse was now on, only I wasn't sure right then who was the cat and who was the mouse. It was a close call.

What I did know was that Mason had done some hard digging and found out that my inheritance could only be touched by my father if I gave him written permission. Or I was deemed incompetent by the state. Since neither had happened, that meant I could claim the money now, and there was nothing my father could do about it with me being over twenty-five.

I'd given Mason permission to file whatever paperwork was required to claim the money. I wasn't sure how much it was or what I'd do with it as I'd never been money hungry. Mason had stated that wasn't the point; it was the fucking principle. My granddaddy had left that money to me, so legally, it was mine.

The car we were in pulled up outside The Mayflower hotel, and I grinned for the first time since we hit the airport at the sight of the doorman's alarmed expression. Mason had to organize several cars to collect us, and some of them had arrived before ours. Men in leather were possibly a rare site at this swanky hotel.

Exiting the car, Sid came out behind me, and the doorman turned and fled into the hotel with a look of alarm on his face.

I chuckled. "Bet you made the guy piss his pants."

Sid glared at the entrance the dude had disappeared through. "Stupid dick."

Linc stepped out next, followed by Mason. The driver got out and took our hand luggage out of the boot, his polite expression never wavering.

Mason tipped the driver and checked what time he'd be back later that afternoon to collect us. When everyone arrived, Mason led us into the hotel with a Linc at his side, giving a 'don't fuck with me' glare at anyone who looked in our direction. The place smelled like rich folks, and those same folks deserted the lobby faster than rats on a sinking ship.

We moved as one toward the large bank of reception desks that was off to the left. The cream marble floor shone. The doomed glass roof above let in light. The area was huge, and the sound of booted feet echoed around us as we made our way over to the reception area.

"I have a reservation under the name of Davenport," Mason said to the petite woman on reception who'd been brave enough to step forward, offering a polite smile.

"Let me just check, Sir," she answered nervously as her hands moved over the keyboard, her gaze repeatedly moving from us to the screen in front of her. "Yes, I see you booked eleven suites, is that correct?"

"It is. Can you confirm breakfast is booked for the morning?"

She swallowed and nodded. "Of course, I'll check now." Several taps later, and she confirmed it was.

It took an hour to get everyone booked in, then we all headed to the rooms with a plan to meet in the bar at lunchtime. All the rooms, as per Mason's request, were on the same floor. Theirs was next to ours, and I nodded to them as Sid opened the door, "Later."

Inside the room, I let out the breath that felt like I'd been holding since we got into the city. The scent, the vibe of the place, left me antsy. Being this close to home in more than five years was...

Sid broke my train of thought as his arms slid around my body, and he pulled me back against him. I met his stare in the mirror that sat right in front of us over the dressing table. "What do you need?"

"To go back to Belton," I answered flippantly.

He sighed and ran a hand over my chest. "We gotta do this. You said it yourself, he ain't gonna leave you alone or us."

I broke free and faced him, my chest heaving. "Don't you think I know that? It just…here." I yanked at my hair. I'd avoided looking out the window of the car at the city that held nothing but bad memories for me. But the view was there right outside the large window. The sun was high, the sky-blue highlighting buildings. Showing me what had once been the place of my nightmares. "The fuckin' memories. There messin' with my head is all."

He came and pulled my hands from my hair, his face pinched with concern. "I got ya back. Hear me. I won't let them touch you. I swear it."

I rested my forehead against his and looked him directly in the eye. "I know. It's not me I'm worried about," I confessed before pressing a kiss to his lips, needing something more than words.

Chapter 25

SID

The rate at which my heart was beating, I wasn't sure I wouldn't pass out at some point when the car stopped in front of the gates of what could only be described as a mansion.

"You grew up here?" The disbelieve I could hear in my voice couldn't be helped. The reality of where Toad came from was like being hit with a hammer. It left me more than a little dazed.

Toad didn't look out the window, staring straight ahead. "Yes and no. I lived here till they realized I was gay. After that, it was mostly hospital wards." His voice held no emotion.

Mason gave me a worried look, and I shook my head, trying to convey Toad would be okay, even when I wasn't sure. After he'd fucked me hard against the wall, we'd gone down for lunch and sat with everyone, but he hadn't said a word. His expression closed off, and it sent chills down my body. Would he cope facing his father?

There was no way of knowing, and now there was no turning back. As planned, we'd left the hotel and got back into the hired car Mason had arranged to take us to Hanna's house. Mr. Hanna had agreed to a meeting a little too easy for my liking, but Mason was confident that things would go our way.

The briefcase tucked next to his leg on the floor held a wealth of information he'd shared with everyone. Mr. Hanna had his fingers a lot of *dirty* pies. The guy made Dark Angels look whiter than white. It caused my stomach to feel like I'd been living on pure caffeine ever since. Linc believed in Mason, so I had to trust that he was right and that he'd be able to get rid of the monkey of Toad's back.

The driver opened his window and leaned out to press a button to call for attention.

A tinny voice asked, "What is your business here?"

Mason shifted closer to the open window. "It's Mr. Davenport. I have an appointment with Mr. Hanna at three pm. He's expecting us."

"Please wait." There was a click then silence followed.

Two minutes later, the electronic gates in front of us opened. I glanced behind us to check they didn't shut before the other vehicles following us got through the gate.

Mason glanced at the silent Toad. "You ready?"

"As I'll ever be," he muttered as the car stopped in front of a set of white marble steps.

Unsure what I'd expected or truly understood about where Toad came from, the house was one thing. The dude dressed in black, looking like he had a dead fish under his nose, was something else entirely. "Is that a fuckin' butler?"

"It is. Marsh has been with the family since I can remember." Once more, Toad's voice gave none of his emotions away.

Another look of concern passed between Mason and Linc before Linc opened the door and exited the vehicle. The butler dude's expression remained the same as the drive filled with men all dressed for what I knew to be battle. The flight had ensured that none of the usual weapons we used could travel with us. But none of the men or women were worried about that. There wasn't a member who hadn't proven they could fight when needed.

Mason only approached the steps once everyone was out of the cars. Linc had been clear no one, including Mason, was to be left in a position of vulnerability. If anyone wanted to take a leak, they'd have to wait until we left.

We all flanked Toad forming a protective circle as we followed Mason up the steps. Toad was to remain protected at all times so no one could pull a surprise attack on him.

"Sir, I'm led to believe it was just you and Master Mark who would be attending the meeting."

I gritted my teeth together at the warning look Linc fired at me. Mason was to do all the talking, for now.

"Then there has been a misunderstanding. I apologize. As you can see, we are here now. Shall we proceed?"

The butler, for the first time, showed some uncertainty as Mason stepped around him and walked toward the open door with utter confidence. Taking this as an opportunity, none of us waited for an invitation or the butler to argue. The sounds of boots thumping against the marble echoed in the large house as we entered. The scent of lemons and something sweeter I couldn't name was all but overpowering as I stopped to stare.

There was more marble—black this time—and it glittered in the sunlight pouring out of the high windows behind us. The place felt cold and impersonal. There were no pictures on the walls, but two sculptures of nude women stood on either side of the large staircase that Scarlett O'Hara would have been proud of.

A cough and a sniff came after the door shut behind us. "Please wait here." His shoes clopped over the floor as the butler disappeared down the long hallway to the left.

"Where will your father be right now?" Mason asked the second the guy disappeared from sight.

"He'll be in his study if he's still a creature of habit." Toad nodded in the direction in which the butler had gone. "It's down that hallway and off to the left."

"Lead on," Linc said, "but remember to stay close to Sid."

Toad gave a curt nod as his chest heaved, and he went in the direction he'd just indicated. He'd got no more than several steps when a group of large men appeared at the end of the hallway. Dressed in black suits, they formed what I suspected they thought was an intimidating wall. I counted eight men as they stood saying nothing before a tall, slim man appeared and stood in front of them.

The arrogant expression identified who he was even before Toad stiffened next to me. "Mark, why do you always have to be so troublesome." The man's gaze flickered over us, then dismissed us. "You were always prone to the dramatics and have now got these...men involved in your unrealities." He sniffed and shook his head as if he was talking about something as asinine as the weather.

"Really, my unrealities. Is that what we're now calling being gay, *Father*?" Only the last word held any kind of infliction as Toad's jaw bunched, his hands flexing at his sides as if readying to punch the fucker in front of him.

The need to touch him wouldn't be quelled, and I sucked in a deep breath while reaching for his hand. It was clammy as he twisted toward me, eyes widening for a second before he took my hand and clung to it. His Adam's apple repeatedly bobbed, gratefulness there in the depth of his gaze as it locked with mine. Wordlessly I opened up to him, letting him see I was there for him, for whatever he needed—not just now—forever.

Several seconds passed before Toad gave a slight nod, the only indication he understood as he turned back toward his father when he gritted out, "you mention that filth into my home, then wave the profanity under my nose. You have the nerve to question my reality. Your perversions need to be dealt with."

He hadn't finished speaking when another man appeared, this one looking more than a little uncomfortable as he fidgeted, looking nervously at everyone. Around fifty, his hair all gray, the suit he wore was crumpled looking next to Mr. Hanna's immaculate suit.

Mr. Hanna glanced at the man. "As you can see, Dr. Slater, he's still in denial about the obvious issues with his mental state. Therefore he's clearly unable to make any rational decisions for himself. Those will need to be left to—"

I'd had enough of this bullshit nonsense. "Shut the fuck up. Don't you fuckin' dare," I growled low and mean at Dr. Slater, making sure to add all the menace I felt in each word, "pull that shit. There is

238

fuck all wrong with your son." I held up our joint hands. "Lovin' a guy isn't a fuckin' perversion. What's perverse is you. Pull your fuckin' head out of your ass and join the fuckin' twenty-first century. Who folks chose to love has got fuck all to do with bein' rational. I'm sure your wife can attain to that. She fell for your ludicrous ass, that shows she ain't fuckin' rational."

There was some sniggering, and I wasn't convinced it only came from the men flanking me. The grip on my hand increased, but I kept my eye on the man who looked like he might stroke out at any time.

Mason held up his hand. "I think we've gotten off on the wrong foot." His voice was all smooth as silk, but the hint of steel was unmistakable when he stepped forward. He opened his briefcase and offered a sheet of paper. "Maybe it would be in your best to read this first, then consider your next decision carefully."

Linc growled at the two men that came toward Mason. "Touch him, and you'll never walk again."

Mason fired a wicked grin back at Linc before glancing back at Mr. Hanna, who was looking a little less arrogant as he read what he held.

The man, who I suspected was a psychiatric doctor, shifted and shoved his trembling hands into the pockets of his suit jacket. I eyed him. "Take a hike. You ain't needed."

Mr. Hanna remained tight-lipped when the guy looked between Hanna and me. He hesitated. "Mr. Hanna, I'm not sure...Mark appears—"

"*Mark* is normal. I was the first time you assessed me. What does the old man have on you? Whatever it is, we've got more on him. Your lies today won't be required." The anger whipped out of Toad and hit its target when the man cringed.

He then sagged, giving Toad a look of what seemed to be regret. "Yes, I'm sorry." He didn't look at Toad's father. This time there was no hesitation as he fled past us as if the devil were chasing him. Was the doc just a pawn in all this too?

I didn't get a chance to dwell on it as Mason asked politely, "Shall we continue this meeting here? Or in your office?"

"My office," Mr. Hanna bit out. The icy anger directed at Toad left me closing the tiny bit of distance between us. I pulled him flush against my body and gave his old man a toothy grin.

The disgust was there in the curl of his lip, but he kept his thoughts to himself this time. The men shifted back as Mr. Hanna swung around and stalked off, his posture stiff.

"He got a stick up his ass to walk like that?" I murmured next to Toad's ear.

"If he hasn't, he needs one to clear the shit out of him." There was no humor in the reply, but he did attempt to smile, though it didn't reach his eyes.

Mason, the first to move, walked after the group of men that followed Mr. Hanna. Linc threw a frustrated look at Mason, marching after him. A ripple of unease ran through me as we entered a room nearly the size of the whole of the clubhouse. Cigar smoke and leather the undertones that met my nose as I inhaled. The man now seated behind the large mahogany desk with a wall of books behind him exposed his hatred. The bodyguards ranged around the room with two stood, one on either side of the still open office door. I indicated to Dex, Ram, and Razor to stand to block the doorway.

Once they'd moved, I gave my full attention to Toad's father.

Chapter 26

TOAD

The familiar scents assailed my senses as I clung unashamedly to Sid. Being in this room brought back nothing but dreadful memories I didn't want to recall, not now, not ever. The presence of the club members, of Sid's hand in mine, was the only reason I was able to hold the old bastard's stare when it lifted from the sheet of paper Mason had given him.

He hadn't been fast enough to hide the shock when he'd first read what he held. It was a small victory, but I took it when I'd had so few in the past. Although I wasn't stupid enough to underestimate him. He'd proven more cunning than a fox in a hen house. Dr. Slater hadn't changed much since the last time I'd seen him. It had given me a nasty jolt seeing him appear, and I couldn't say I wasn't unhappy that he'd run like the fucking coward he was.

I'd never figured what the old man had on him, but it must be something bad if he could manipulate him enough to get him to risk his license to practice.

The paper fluttered to the desk. He sat back in the leather chair, like a king in his fuckin' castle. Only the twitching muscle in his jaw gave away his fury. "What is the purpose of this," his bony finger pointed to the piece of paper, "information?"

"I think we can cut out the bullshit. That list pertains to the documents I have in my possession that implicate you with, let's say, several business deals that wouldn't take close scrutiny from those that you've been rubbing shoulders with politically." The smile that followed was anything but pleasant. "And of course, there is the little matter of tax evasion." Mason tapped at his lower lip as if thinking. "There is also the misappropriation of funds from three companies. I'm sure the board of directors wouldn't be too happy to hear about where you've been spending their money." Mason looked at the other men around the room as if bored.

Slowly the high color in my father's cheeks lessened as the hand on the desk curled into a fist. "Are you threatening me?"

"Why, of course not. Just like you wouldn't be making any threats toward my client, now would you? I think we can sort out this little mess satisfactorily, don't you?" Mason gave him no chance to answer. "Your pursuit of your son is to cease immediately."

There was no mention of the attempted kidnapping because Mason wasn't fully aware of what had happened to the two men. Some things would never be shared with Mason, and that was one of them. He'd argued with Linc, but he'd held firm. His explanation about putting Mason's career in jeopardy had worked, but that meant Mason couldn't use it. On balance with everything else, it had been agreed it let that slide.

Another piece of paper appeared out of the briefcase and was laid on the desk. Right after, a large file appeared and was placed next to the paper. The file held duplicate copies of all the information that proved Mason wasn't bluffing.

"The file," Mason nodded toward what he'd placed down, "has duplicates of everything I've mentioned." This time Mason pointed to the sheet of paper. "Sign that, and all your problems will go away. You'll never hear from my friends or me again. That is as long as you stick to the binding agreement." There weren't any niceties now. His expression clearly revealed his thoughts as he waited for the stoic man in front of him to respond.

Would he sign it? Would he agree to free me from the chains he'd tried to hold me with? The air got stuck somewhere between my mouth and chest and refused to budge as I watched the man whose hate I'd never understood open the file. A quick scan was all it took for the full fury to appear in bulging neck veins and the now dark-red face.

I wasn't spared a glance as he put the file down with trembling fingers to reach for the legal agreement that laid out explicitly that there was nothing wrong with my mental health. That I could inherit without him coming after me with some bullshit claim about my state of mind.

His only reaction as he lifted a pen and scrawled over the bottom of the page was to arch one brow.

"This ends all connections."

"It does. Mark, Toad, doesn't use his surname and has no intention of ever revealing his...connection to you. That bit of paper ensures that all parties are protected. That Toad receives what is rightfully his, and it puts an end to the vendetta you have against your son for his 'gayness'." Mason's voice was full of disgust.

The man never glanced in my direction as he held the sheet of paper, offering it to Mason. "Make sure he sticks to the agreement."

The chuckle was anything but humorous as Mason took the paper, glancing at it quickly, then tucking it back into his briefcase. His gaze moved back to the man. "I don't think you'll have any worries there. Who'd want to be willingly associated with a bigoted asshole, who can't see the value of all human beings, especially his own son?" Mason leaned over the desk. "People like you make me sick to my stomach. You're a fucking disgrace. Your son is a wonderful man, and saying he's got mental health problems because he's gay says more about you and your own repressed nature. I'd think about that if I were you."

He stood back and swung to face Linc, who didn't get time to respond when Mason grabbed hold of his neck with his free hand and kissed him hard and fast. "Love is special and should be treasured as the gift it is," he said loud enough for all to hear, his gaze never moving from Linc's.

"Get out of my home," the man, who'd never been any kind of father to me, shouted from behind the desk. His eyes wild.

"What no goodbye hug, no 'I'll miss you, son.' You know I was terrified of coming here today to confront you. But what you are is sick. You're the one who needs a psych bed." I sucked in a deep breath, needing a moment to say my own mental goodbye. "The universe has a way of reflecting back what anyone gives out. I don't even need to hang around to know one day you'll get yours."

"I said get out of my home," he screamed, spit landing on the desk in front of him.

Mason gave him a dismissive glance. "Gladly."

Exactly a minute later, we were all outside the now-closed gates, some wearing disappointed expressions. In contrast, others joked about Mason being a badass. I stared up at the place I'd spent my childhood, trying to recall a happy time. Was it sad and pathetic that I could think of none?

I shuddered against Sid, who remained, holding me close. Sid exchanged a look with Linc, and he nodded before Sid growled, "Let's get the fuck out of here and go home."

☠ ☠ ☠

There was little I remembered of the return trip to Belton. My head wasn't up for functioning with everything swirling around inside it in one glorious fucked up mess. Had my father really agreed to the terms Mason had laid out, or was he just fucking with us?

He signed the paperwork. It was legal and binding. Was it really over?

It was way too anticlimactic, leaving me with nothing to confirm it was real, that he would now leave me to live my life, my way.

I shut my eyes and willed myself to go to sleep. Sid's warm body shifted to press solidly against my back. His arm came over the sheet, and a hand lay on my uneasy stomach. "What's up?" He mumbled sleepily in my ear.

"Nothin'. Go back to sleep."

"I'm awake," he answered, sounding only half-awake.

"I'm good—"

He moved away, and the light came on next to the bed. He shifted to sit up against the wooden headboard, a hand rubbing over his bristly jaw.

"You ain't been good since we left that shithole that was once your home. Talk to me."

I'd have been able to resist him if he'd been angry, but the concern he was expressing gave me no place to hide. "I never stuck it to him," I blurted out without realizing that was what had been playing on my mind. "I didn't really get to lay out how he really made me feel."

Sid came forward and all but lifted me onto his chest before settling back again. A fluttering started in the center of my chest as he secured his arms around me. He laid his chin on my head, his chest rising and falling slowly. "Then tell me."

Was it that simple? I wasn't sure, but what other option did I have?

None.

I shut my eyes and willed back the hot ache that developed behind my eyes. "When I took off from the hospital, I kinda shut out the past like it didn't happen. I think it was the only way I could survive at the time. Drifting from place to place, trying to keep below his radar, I let myself believe I was normal. That I didn't have a lunatic for an old man."

"Got the same T-shirt," Sid muttered, his hand running up and down my back gently.

He was right. Maybe it was why I'd been drawn to him because I sensed a kindred spirit? "Yeah, I suppose we do. What would you say to your old man now?" I shifted so I could see his face.

He gave a shrug, though he looked like he was considering his answer when his brow furrowed. "I have nothin' to say to him because he ain't worth it. He was a scumbag. Nothin' changes that. I can't alter what happened. Hell, if I know whether it would make a difference to how I am now." His hands cupped my face, his eyes full of emotions. "One thing I do know, you make me see things differently. See what matters most, and not some useless talk about shit I can't change."

I chuckled at how put-out he sounded. "You'll set my heart a flutterin' with your flowery words."

"Fuck off," he said even as his lips tugged into a smile and the knots unraveled in my gut.

I returned his smile. "See, who says romance is dead."

"I'll show you romance." He flipped me, and I landed on my back more than a little breathless from the scorching desire aimed at me. His large body pinned me to the bed, and my now firming cock pressed against his. "You gonna let me fuck you?"

Exhaling at the need, I nodded, unable to speak past the desire.

His lips claimed mine, and the kiss was endless and full of all the emotions my man struggled to voice. Familiar hands stroked over my body with a possessiveness that ensured I was fully aroused before he released my mouth so he could kiss his way down my body. His lips worshiped me, his tongue lighting paths of fire that led straight to my groin. Precum cooled on my skin as he threw back the covers and worked to drive me mad before his lips wrapped around my cock. Saliva dripped over my balls and down my taint, his fingers following the path.

Warm, wet fingers pressed against me, and I bore down as he pushed a finger deep inside. The burn got a loud moan that seemed to please Sid as he increased the suction on my cock. More saliva dripped down my sac, and Sid used it to stretch me. One finger became two, then three until I could do no more than grunt out curses when he didn't stop until I hung on the edge of wanting to shoot into the wet, heavenly mouth trying to suck my brains out of my cock.

"Fuck me, stop teasin'."

His chuckle vibrated up my cock, and I had to forcibly will back the need to come. Seconds later, his mouth released me, and I breathed a little easier until he shifted and his mouth took mine in a brutal kiss. Our teeth clashed together as his tongue delved into my mouth in a wet hungry duel for dominance.

Breathless and lightheaded, he finally released my mouth. His chest billowed as his eyes glittered. "Gonna let me fuck you bare?"

We'd stopped using condoms, but as yet, Sid hadn't had the opportunity to fuck me without one. "Fuck, yeah." My desperation was at an all-time high, and right then, I wasn't sure how long I'd last when his cock got inside me.

As if he'd read my mind, he reached over me to grab the bottle of lube he kept in the bedside drawer. I shut my eyes, breathing deep, working on regaining control. The sound of the snick was followed by a slick hand running down the length of my cock, taking away the little bit of control I'd gained.

I cursed. "Stop fuckin' about and get that cock inside me," I ground out impatiently as his slicked fingers ran over my sensitive skin.

A wicked glint appeared as he bared his teeth. Two fingers pushed inside me an inch, then he held them still. "You beggin'?"

"Shit! Yes." It came out more like a groan, but I didn't care when he replaced his fingers with his cock. One hand stroked my cock while he slowly, inch by torturous inch, sank into my body. My ass clenched down, increasing the burn, the stretch so good.

Sweat slid down the side of his face as he worked to keep it slow. Only when he was fully seated inside me did he look up from where our bodies joined. His body still, emotions, too many to name, ran through me, and I reached up to cup his face. "I love you."

There was a flash of pure joy, then he was kissing me. His hands, cock, and lips working to make it impossible to do anything other than feel. We rolled over the bed until I was straddling his hips, my hands pressing against his heart that beat hard and fast. His large hands held me as he repeatedly thrust into my body.

The angle so perfect cum spurted out of my untouched cock, landing over his chest less than a minute later. As my ass clamped down on his cock, his head pushed into the mattress, his neck muscles straining. Heat filled my ass as I collapsed forward in a sweaty heap against his chest, gasping for breath.

His hands eventually released their punishing grip on my hips to drape over my sweaty back, pressing me closer. Cum spread between us as my head rose and fell with each rapid breath he took.

Long minutes passed before I had enough energy to lift my head. Sid's eyes were closed. "You know this talkin' shit, there's a lot to be said for it."

He chuckled, his eyes slit open. "That there is."

I pressed a kiss to the skin I could reach and settled my head on his shoulder.

"You good?"

I nestled in and shut my eyes, giving myself a minute to think about it. Was I good? "Yeah, yeah, I think I am. Thanks."

"Any time," he whispered before his lips brushed over the top of my head.

A smile spread over my face as my ass twinged when his cock slipped free. "Yeah, but maybe next time we'll stick to the talkin' or me fuckin' you."

My head was dislodged as he barked out a loud laugh. "Don't like it rough? Try rememberin' that when you got me pinned to a wall."

The last time I'd done that had been in the hotel in D.C. "I don't remember you complainin' at the time."

He shifted, and darkness descended as he muttered, "Shut up and go to sleep."

Chapter 27

SID

Toad held my attention. He was hard to read as he sat on the edge of the bed staring at the message that had pulled us from sleep.

"What's up?"

His gaze moved from the phone to me and then back. "Mason wants me to go to his office this morning."

"Think it's about your inheritance?" Toad had been asked to sign some stuff the week before to legally obtain access to his money. He'd gone alone to see Mason and hadn't mentioned anything since. There'd been no fall out as yet from the visit to D.C., and at times I wasn't sure if we were holding our breaths collectively, waiting for what would come next.

Over that, I'd tried my damnedest not to think about the differences between our pasts, but it was hard when I recalled the house he'd grown up in. I tried to look at the place objectively, but I didn't have a clue what living in that kind of place would be like.

He wasn't loved, same as you. As the thought filtered past the worry, I reached out to him. No one had loved him, same as me. Family had placed restrictions on that—we weren't different—fuck, we were the same, just lived in different places.

He took my hand and used it to rub at the side of his bristly cheek. "Think so. You wanna come with me?"

The tightness across the top of my shoulders eased at his offer even as the uncertainty I could hear gave me the jitters. "Yep. I don't have anything going on that can't wait an hour or two."

The warm imprint of his hand lingered as he removed it to send a reply. The cell phone bounced on the bed as he dropped it. Getting up, he sauntered naked to the bathroom without looking back.

I called after him, "Want company?"

He glanced back over his shoulder, a sexy smirk gracing his gorgeous face. "When do you ever need to ask that?" He chuckled, wiggled his ass at me, then disappeared into the bathroom.

Up and running a second later, he laughed as I burst through the door eagerly.

The shower lasted much longer than normal, with him deciding that shower sex was required after he'd sucked my cock dry. My ass twinged as I dried off and dressed, my gaze moving back repeatedly to the man doing the same. There'd been no mention of him moving back to his own place, and I was loath to bring it up if he decided that's what he wanted to do. If the threat was really gone, then there was no reason why he'd need to remain at my place. Had he realized that?

"You got your thinkin' face on. What's up?"

"Nothin'." His brows rose as he stopped in the process of zipping up his jeans. His chest held a few droplets of water from his hair that hung around his attractive face. "You plannin' on headin' back to your apartment?" It was out before I could stop myself.

The deep furrows that appeared around his eyes and mouth gave me a dose of nervous energy. I swung around to sit on the edge of the bed to pull on my boots, all the while avoiding looking in Toad's direction. A second later, a hand landed on my shoulder, and I sighed.

"You want me to leave?" His voice revealed nothing of what he was feeling.

I glanced up and met his stare. I sucked in a shaky breath and opted for the truth. "Nope, I want you to give up your lease and move in here with me." I'd never wanted that with anyone in my life, but I now couldn't imagine him not being here: in my home, in my life.

The grin was as bright as the Texas sun and just as hot. "I'd like that." He swooped down, his lips hard and wet as he kissed me with a passion that never failed to wake up my whole fucking body.

Seconds later, he walked off whistling while my cock ached and my heart flipped cartwheels in my chest. "Cruel fucker," I shouted after him as I thumped at my cock.

"And don't you love it," he called back.

"Fuck yeah," I muttered, not loud enough for him to hear.

💀 💀 💀

The relaxed breakfast we had at a café in Killeen now seemed a distant memory as we strolled into Mason's office. Toad seemed to have taken to fidgeting and hadn't stopped playing with his cell phone as it moved from one hand to the next.

"Have a seat. You want coffee?" Mason asked while he stood holding the office door.

"No, we're cool," I answered for both of us when Toad didn't appear to hear the question.

The door clicked shut, and Mason walked over to his desk. His brow quirked up at me as his head tilted toward Toad. The *is everything all right* look got a shoulder shrug. We'd been fine, laughing and messing around right up until we'd entered the building.

"Sit, please. This won't take too long." As he spoke, Mason sat behind his desk and pulled a file toward him. His lips pursed.

I waited for Toad to choose one of the two seats in front of Mason's desk. As he sank into the one directly in front of Mason, he asked, "Did he sign everything off?"

Mason gave him a confident smile. "Did you doubt me last week?"

Toad's chuckle was without humor. "I've known him a lot longer than you. He's never known for his honesty."

I remained silent but reached out and took hold of his hand, interlinking our fingers. Toad always got a funny grin on his face when I did that, and it appeared now. A fluttering in my chest followed. Sappy fuck!

"As I explained, the legal document he signed when we were in D.C. ensures that if he so much as makes a move in your direction, a shit storm will rain down on him." Mason opened the file and took at several pieces of paper. "The paperwork, as discussed, was filed, and the money was transferred this morning to the designated account number you gave me." His gaze lifted to us as he held out papers to Toad. "It's done. You're free."

Toad's fingers clenched mine until I lost the circulation to them. "Seriously...it's...done." His voice was thick with tears, and when I met his gaze, his eyes sparkled in the morning light coming in through the window behind Mason.

"You're free." I lifted his hand and kissed his fingers in a move I'd be mortified about later, but right then, it seemed like the right thing to do.

A lone tear slid down his cheek. "How much was it?"

Mason coughed and dropped the papers on the desk when Toad showed no sign of taking them. "Three-point-two million dollars after the taxes and transfer fees."

"Holy fuck," I choked out around a throat that was trying to close up.

Toad sat forward, pulling me with him as he put his phone down and finally reached for the paperwork. "Shit, what the fuck am I supposed to do with that?"

Mason laughed, a big hearty sound as he slapped at his desk. "Spend it, enjoy it. Do something crazy to stick it to the old man."

Toad's gaze skimmed over the papers instead of answering Mason as if he couldn't quite believe what the other man had said. When he finally lifted his head, his eyes were wide and looked a little wild. "I'll need to...give this some thought." His hand trembled as he placed the papers back on Mason's desk.

"You can do what the heck you want. It's done. Nothing is tying you to your family. You are free, Mark."

Toad jerked when Mason emphasized his name.

Minutes later, we were outside the building and heading back to the truck I'd borrowed.

Toad remained silent until we were back in the cab of the truck. "It's a lot of money. Does it make a difference...to you...to us?"

The hesitation ate at me as I didn't have a clue how to read what was going on in his mind because he'd avoided looking at me when he'd spoken. "Look at me." I waited until he did. "I got money. I got more than I need. Linc has seen to that by makin' me a partner in the business." I winked at him. "You helped with your custom jobs. Money ain't an issue unless you make it one. I couldn't give a rat's ass what you got in the bank. It ain't my business unless you wanna buy me a 1936 Knucklehead, then I won't say no." I joked, hoping to lessen the tension that had developed between us.

His head tipped back, and he released a loud belly laugh. My lips twitched as he rocked in the seat for more than a minute before he got control of himself. "Okay, it's a done deal as you're easily pleased."

This time it was me laughing as I tugged him against me and kissed him hard and fast. Both of us breathless when I pulled back. "I got what I want, you. I don't need nothin' else." I pressed a gentle kiss against his lips when he released a soft sigh. The air thickened, and I kissed him once more, slow and easy. His lips parted, and his tongue slid against mine as he moaned. His lips clung to mine, but neither of us fought for dominance. It was something new and scary. Yet, it left me happier than I'd ever been in my life.

"I love you," I whispered against his lips.

"I know."

Chapter 28

I wasn't sure what was worse, listening to Dex go on about his girlfriend's antics in the bedroom or avoiding Sid for fear I'd let something slip. I was sure he suspected I was up to something by the deep furrow that had been permanently between his brows over the last week. A week since I'd taken possession of my birthday gift for him.

Last month, after we'd visited Mason's office and I suddenly became a millionaire, I hadn't been able to shake Sid's throw-away comment about his dream motorcycle. An idea had taken root when Linc brought up the date of Sid's birthday, and it hadn't let go. So I'd done my research on the Knucklehead, the price was a breath-taking hundred thousand dollars, but it was the bike that had inspired the teardrop tank that was a dream to put artwork on. One look at the motorcycle on the internet, and I'd been sold with my head full of how I could personalize it for Sid.

The long-held promise I'd do a custom paint job had changed from his hog to the Knucklehead. In two days, it was Sid's birthday, and I'd been keeping my plans on the down-low with the exception of Linc and Mason. I was using their garage to store the motorcycle I'd bought three weeks ago and had delivered last week. Linc had taken the tank off the hog so it didn't arouse any suspicion. It was in the auto shop, dropped off by Linc when Sid had gone out to get some parts.

I'd been secretly working on painstakingly painting the design I'd originally done for Sid's hog on the old tank. The prep work took time, and with Sid just on the other side of the plastic, it left me a bag of nerves. How had I not noticed how often Sid liked to come over and chat with me while I worked?

The man was like a bloodhound, sniffing out that I was doing something for him. He appeared every fucking time I started to touch the tank. It was driving me to distraction. At this rate, I'd never have the tank finished and put back on the hog by Friday.

"She pulls this kind of yoga move—"

I slapped my hand over Dex's mouth as it registered where the conversation was going. "Do

I go into graphic detail about where my cock goes?" I asked in frustration.

Dex's bushy eyebrows shot up his forehead as his eyes traveled to Sid, who was seated at the bar talking to Tina. He shook his head, dislodging my hand. "Yeah, right, okay, no more sexy talk."

"Thanks."

Dex picked up his beer and drank deep before switching topics. "You done anything with your money yet?"

It was no secret how much I'd inherited. If folks asked, I was honest. I'd given Linc enough money to cover the trip to D.C., feeling it was only right to replace the funds. He hadn't argued. Instead he'd used it to fund this month's ride out, which was planned for this weekend to coincide with Sid's forty-third birthday.

"Not much," I answered when Sid glanced in our direction. It was hard to keep the excitement to myself. The Knucklehead was every Harley rider's wet dream. When talk turned to motorcycles, this one was often mentioned. I was sure that a few of the guys were going to cream their pants when they got a load of Sid's present. Linc had, he'd sat on it and given Mason a look that would have melted the asphalt when the other man had come to see what we were up to. Mason wasn't all that keen on riding pillion, and Linc often teased him about it after Mason had complained that Linc turned into a maniac when he rode the hog.

"You don't have anything you've dreamed of ownin'?" Dex's eyes gleamed with excitement. "I always wanted to go to the large Harley-Davison showroom in Austin and walk out decked out in all their fancy gear."

I chewed on my lip, the wheels in my head turning as I eyed those in the clubhouse. These were my family; they'd proven that they'd stand for me. Family shared the wealth. "Is that what you'd do with enough cash?"

Dex blinked slowly, a dreamy look on his face. "Yeah."

"That's all, you wouldn't do anythin' else?"

He shook his head, finished his drink, then got up. "Nope. I'm a simple man with simple tastes...except when it comes to leather."

"Will you stop that crap?" I shuddered.

He laughed and scratched his head. "Sorry." He raised his bottle and shook it. "Want another?"

I shook my head, and he walked off to the bar, leaving me with my thoughts. Another idea formed about what some of the other cash could be used for. Was it stupid to waste the cash on gifts? The memory of how often my father had penny-pinched when it came to gifts but not to lavish parties pushed me out of the seat. It was easier than I'd anticipated getting folks to talk about things they'd like if they had the cash to splash around. Most of the members worked for businesses Linc owned, and those who didn't, worked for Razor. There were only a couple of them, like Matt, who worked for themselves.

Linc was generous and made sure none of the members were left to struggle finically. It was one of the many things that I admired about Linc. He was a solid president; he tolerated no bullshit or fools. No one got a second chance to cross him.

As the evening wore on, I made a mental list of what people wanted. By the time I made it to where Sid was, ever watchful from his barstool, he had a serious expression on his face.

He nodded in the direction of the room behind me. "What you doin'?"

I grinned at him. "Gathering intel."

Tina, who was pulling a beer, laughed. "Intel. Love it, but the only thing you'll get from this bunch is a ball ache."

"Now that's where you're wrong." I slid onto the stool next to Sid and rested my elbows on the bar, my chin on my hand. "Did you know that Cammy likes to sketch in pastels and wants a Scottish artist named Angela Davison to make him an original piece of artwork of his trusted beagle? Or that Tink has a passion for collecting sports memorabilia and can recite the history of baseball?"

Her eyes widened. "You've been a busy boy."

"I have. So what is your secret yearnin'?"

She laughed. "Fuck if I know. I don't have any hidden passions." Her shoulders shrugged as her expression became thoughtful. "Sounds daft, but

I've always wanted one of those pamper days in one of those fancy spas in Austin. You know the places where they do secret things to your body to make you feel ten years younger."

Adding that to the list, I gave her an answering grin. "Nice."

Sid twisted his body to look at me. "What's this about?"

I leaned in and whispered in his ear. "Giving."

His brows arched as confusion appeared in his eyes. "Giving?"

"That's what I said." I indicated to the bottles behind Tina on the shelf. "I'll have a Jameson. You want one, Sid?"

He rubbed a hand over his bald head. "What's gotten into you? And yeah, I'll have one. We can get a cab home."

"Nothin' got into me...*yet*."

Tina groaned. "Don't, you're my brothers, I do not need to have those images in my head...okay...maybe."

"Shut up," Sid growled.

Taking that he meant both of us, I made a motion of zipping my lips as Tina went to get our drinks.

"Tell me what you're up to," Sid persisted when Tina laid the drinks on the bar, took the cash, and then served Ram, who had sat on a stool next to Razor.

"Dex gave me an idea while he was chatterin' on about his girl."

"He did?" There was disbelief as Sid shifted to look at Dex then back at me.

"Yep, he was asking what I was going to do with the cash."

"That ain't none of his business."

Before he could get into rant mode, I laid a hand on top of his and squeezed. "He wasn't being nosey, just more excited for me to do somethin' with it. And it's been a month and the only thing..." I swallowed the words before I could trip myself up, rushing to think of something else to say, "I've done is cover the expense of going to D.C."

His eyes narrowed as he picked up his glass and sipped at the whiskey.

"Anyway, it got me to thinkin' maybe others' ideas would give me a clue what I wanted to do with the cash." It sounded lame, but it was as close to the truth as I wanted to get right then without Sid asking too many questions that might loosen my lips.

"And did you come up with any ideas?"

I shrugged and picked up my own whiskey. "Maybe," I answered. Taking a sip, I let the whiskey sit on my tongue, enjoying the smooth taste before I swallowed.

Sid's glass thumped against the bar, leaning into me, leaving me no room to move. "You're up to something. I know it, and it's startin' to piss me off. Spill."

The urge to hunch at the accusation was hard to resist when he went all Rambo. Before I could answer, Linc strolled up to the bar, and I gave him a *help me* stare after I'd twisted so Sid couldn't see my pleading eyes.

The twinkle in Linc's eye was the only sign he was finding this funny. He leaned on the bar next to Sid. "I need to go through the figures for last month for the auto shop. I need you to run through them with Nutty, too, before the taxman gets his mitts on the accounts."

Sid threw me a warning look as he slid off the seat, whiskey glass in hand. "We'll talk later." With that, he was gone, and I breathed a little easier.

Now all I needed to do was to keep out of his way for the next forty-eight hours.

Good luck with that!

Chapter 29

SID

Whatever had crawled up Toad's ass over the last week or so had my stomach tied in pretty little bows River would love. My guts, on the other hand, hated them. Toad had gotten drunk Wednesday night at the club, something he rarely did, then yesterday he had a hangover, so he'd had stayed in bed most of the morning. Or so he'd lead me to believe, but when I'd gone up to check on him, the bed had been cold and there'd been no sign of him.

He'd acted like I was the crazy one as he avoided answering any of my questions when he'd finally arrived at the auto shop. He'd then spent the afternoon with a do-not-disturb sign on the outer plastic. That in itself wasn't unusual when he had a motorcycle he was spray painting. Still, I'd checked his schedule, and there'd been nothing booked. None of what was going on made any sense to me, and it was fucking with my head. I trusted and loved him, yet there was niggle of doubt hanging around the edges of my mind that wouldn't shift.

Last night, Toad had gone over to Linc's to speak to Mason, and I had every intention of having it out with him, but I'd fallen asleep before he'd gotten back. The sleepless nights with Toad acting all kinds of weird had whipped my butt.

Then I'd woken to find the bed empty and cold not five minutes ago. The sun was high in the sky, indicating I'd slept in, and my watch had confirmed it. Had Toad not come home last night? A shiver of apprehension ran through me.

Had something happened to him? The legal crap Mason had on his father left the man no loopholes to come at Toad again, but that didn't stop me from checking my phone first to see if I'd had any missed calls or messages. None. Was that a good sign?

I continued to search the apartment, even when I'd sensed I was alone. "Where the fuck is he?" I growled, rubbing at my stomach as I made my way back into the bathroom to grab a shower. It was my fucking birthday, and he hadn't even bothered to...

I swallowed hard and shut down my train of thought when hurt speared my heart. "Fuck him," I muttered even when I didn't mean it. I turned on

272

the shower and thoughtlessly stepped in before it heated up. More curses followed as I rushed to wash.

Focus on the weekend!

Yeah, like that's gonna make it all better.

I stomped out of the shower, dripping water everywhere as I swiped a towel up and carried on into the bedroom, building a head of steam. I got dressed while only partly dry, in too much of a hurry to escape the empty apartment.

The thump of my boots against the stairs was drowned out by the buzzing going on in my ears. My temples throbbed as I exited the door, the anger chasing me all the way.

The sun blinded me for a second, and I stopped to blink, then blinked twice more. My hands lifted to rub at my eyes. Was I having some sort of out-of-body experience? Maybe I was still asleep?

There were several shouts of "Happy birthday" that were loud enough to hurt my eardrums.

Not asleep.

My mouth dried as a surge of excitement rushed through me, so powerful it stole the breath from me and made it impossible to get my lungs to work. That had to be why I squeaked out, "That's a Knucklehead."

The mortification would come later, I was sure, but right then, with Toad's sexy, smug grin aimed at me, I couldn't focus. Toad laid a hand on the tank as Linc, Mason, Ram, Dex, and several of the other Dark Angels grinned like fools at me.

I took a step on shaky legs toward the stunning piece of machinery that I'd jokingly told Toad I wanted. Had he bought this for me? The reality of what was happening sunk in past the shock of seeing my first ever Knucklehead in the flesh. Unable to resist, I ran a finger over the tank. A tank that appeared alive with the colors Toad had used to bring the serpent to life.

They were stunning. The imagery was powerful and captured the attention. Each detail drawing me in for a closer look. The eyes of the serpent seemed to follow me as I took another step closer to what I had never dreamed of owning. An ache developed behind my eyes. I blinked rapidly and swallowed hard when my gaze returned to Toad.

"Fuck...I'm speechless."

Linc laughed. "That's a first. Someone mark that down."

"Funny, not," I muttered as I reached out a hand then drew it back, a little scared to touch again.

Toad came around the back of the hog, dark circles evident as he got closer to me. "Happy birthday."

"Is this what you've been hidin' from me?"

He shuffled his feet and gave a small shrug. "Guilty as charged."

"It's too much."

He shook his head as he took hold of my arms, his expression fierce. "It's not," he snapped, then seemed to draw back. "Fuck, if anything, it's not enough. Accept it for what it is," he pleaded.

My heart thumped hard against my ribs at the adoration, at the love there for all to see. I nodded slowly. "You know I ain't never gonna be able to top this, you get that right?"

He gave me a sassy wink. "You don't need to worry about topping."

"Eww, too much information, man," Ram muttered, his hands rubbing over his face.

Linc slapped his shoulder. "Whatever. We all know you like it any way you can get it." That got several laughs.

"You gonna sit on her or just look at it?" Dex asked, his eyes glowing with lust while staring at my motorcycle.

Toad's brows rose, an impish grin on his lips. "Gonna take me for a ride?"

"Give a dude a chance to look at his new baby," I replied as I shifted closer to the Knucklehead, the excitement winning over my anxiety at touching this prized motorcycle. "Did you know this bike had the biggest influence on Harley's produced since 1936? This beauty is referred to as the father to all modern Harley's. It inspired the air-cooled twins that have been used on bikes ever since."

The guys laughed at my enthusiasm. I ran a hand over the hand-painted tank; the warm metal felt alive. "I think this is your finest piece of artwork."

Toad flushed a bright pink. "Thanks."

Linc nodded. "It's a masterpiece. I'll need to get the professional photographer to come and take some pictures for the website."

"I'm not sure I can replicate this. It was made...from my heart."

Dex made a choking noise. "Can we dispel with all the mushy crap and go tuck into the food Mason brought with him."

There was more chatter before the men all disappeared, leaving me alone with Toad. I lovingly ran my hand over the leather seat that appeared to have been recovered.

Toad pressed his chest to my back, his chin coming to rest on my shoulder as his arms wrapped around my chest. "Do you like your gift?"

"Like, that's like comparin' beer with whiskey. There ain't no comparison, and right now, I can't think of a word that covers how much I love this gift." I twisted my neck to glance at him out the side of my eye. "I love you. I mean it, though. How the fuck does a person top this?"

His lips formed into a devilish smile that got my cock firming. "I might have some ideas about that." His lips pressed to the edge of mine. "Maybe you naked and bent over this beauty would be a good start." His chuckle was downright dirty as the image formed in my mind.

More than a little breathless, I nodded, licking my lips. "That could be arranged." I waited for a beat, then added, "Only if you take good care not to scratch my baby."

His laughter was rich and rippled through me like a sexual caress. "Don't worry, I'm sure I can fix any damage that might be caused to your *baby*," his voice dropped, "when I get you alone later."

There was a shout from Linc, "You gonna come and eat or just stand outside all day?"

I called back, "Gimme a sec." I turned in Toad's arms. "The night you stalked my ass back here, I never told you, but that was the best fuckin' decision you could have made."

His lips twitched. "Is that so?"

"Yep, it is. Look at what you gave me."

There was more twitching as his eyes gleamed with amusement. "The motorcycle?"

I moved until those quivering lips were inches from mine. "No, your heart," I whispered before pressing a soft kiss to his parted lips, capturing the happy sigh.

"You romantic old fool," he murmured.

"Old I'll take...romantic?" I spluttered, feeling heat creep up my neck as I eyed the door behind Toad to make sure no one had heard him. "Not in this lifetime. And don't go spreadin' that shit around. I'll never live it down."

He stepped back and took hold of my hand while rolling his eyes. "Yeah, whatever, but you just sweet nothing'd my ass."

More heat spread up my neck at the obvious truth. "Whatever. Let's grab somethin' to eat." I took another look at the gleaming motorcycle before Toad tugged me toward the door. The ball of emotion lodged in my throat made it hard to speak. "This is the best birthday I ever had."

Toad stopped and stared at me with what looked like the same emotions that were riding through me. "Then I'll need to figure out ways to make sure that ain't the last time you tell me that."

I chuckled. "I can live with that."

Chapter 30

TOAD

"**Y**ou got everything you need?" Sid asked for the umpteenth time.

I had a feeling my level of nervousness was brushing off on him. I pointed to the large stack of envelopes on the kitchen counter. "That's all I need. I've made sure to include all the instructions of how they go about claiming their gift." I chewed on my thumbnail. "You don't think they're gonna think I'm trying to buy them?"

The heartfelt sigh Sid didn't try to disguise put me on the defensive. "It's a genuine question."

"It might be, but you know everyone. You know that they all have your back. Why would any of them think you're tryin' to buy them? I don't think that when you lavish me with gifts."

I'd only given him...two motorcycles. I rubbed at my face. "You're different, you're my guy."

"I know, and so does my ass that's twingin' right now."

Laughter rumbled through me. "You said harder," I accused through my chuckling.

"Yeah, whatever. We aren't talkin' about that." His cheeks were turning a deep shade of red right before he walked to the stack on the counter and picked it up. "Everyone will get what you're doin'. You have a huge heart, Toad, one that they will all appreciate." He shrugged. "And if they don't, then they'll deal with me."

"Can it, Rambo. I'm not lookin' to cause a fight tonight." Sid had gotten way too protective of me over the last couple of months. One of the newer prospects had threatened me, and before I could deal with it, Sid had knocked the guy's lights out. He'd then been kicked out of the club. No one crosses a brother. It was a hard rule and one the guy was aware of.

As if he'd read my thoughts, he shook his head. "That dude had been askin' for it. It wasn't like he didn't know you're mine." I raised one brow. "You are. Just as I'm yours."

The justification made my stomach flutter even as I shook my head. "Let's go before we're late because I need to show you I'm yours in the bedroom."

His body shuddered, and his eyes hooded as he stepped toward me. I held up my hands, laughing.

"You gonna explain to Linc why we're late?" That stopped him, and I pushed the disappointment to one side, with thoughts that we'd pick this back up later.

We were out the door with a rucksack slung over my back as I rode my hog to the clubhouse with Sid riding his CVO Street Glide Harley, it was the second bike I'd bought him. It was a limited edition hotrod model. They'd only made three-and-a-half thousand of them.

I'd become a little addicted to Sid's reaction whenever he spoke about motorcycles.

The powerful touring bike had a V-Twin engine and the sound was pure music. The setting sun caught all the gleaming chrome as he weaved past me and took off down the highway toward the clubhouse.

An hour later, as everyone poured into church, the nerves took hold of my stomach and threatened to derail the three months of hard work to figure out how to get everyone what they wanted. Linc gave me a nod once everyone had sat down to indicate the floor was mine.

As I strived to swallow past the dryness in my mouth, I stood up, drawing everyone's attention to me. Linc had organized this meeting on the pretense that there was some business to discuss about the list of new prospects that had grown over the last month. The list was on the agenda, but not really why everyone had been called tonight. The final confirmation email on the piece of artwork I'd commissioned had come through yesterday, meaning that everything was now in place for me to reveal what I'd been up to.

Sid gave me an encouraging smile, one that was there more often than not of late. He'd said in private that I'd made him soft. I begged to differ on that; he was still a scary motherfucker when riled. But I'd secretly agreed that his edges weren't as rough as when I'd first met him.

The chatter died down. I licked at my lips and shoved my trembling hands into my jean pockets as I figured out where to start. "Some of you might not know, but it was Sid that brought me to Belton. I saw him in a bar in Austin and—"

"No, we don't need to know," Ram said, placing his hands over his ears, making everyone laugh.

"Hey, speak for yourself," Nutty said loud enough she could be heard over the laughter. Her eyes glinting with mischievous.

I worked to keep the heat from climbing its way up my neck. "Yeah, right. Anyway, I moved here and found something I wasn't expecting...*family*. Found acceptance that I'd never had my entire life." My voice broke, and I shut my eyes for a second to pull myself together. When I opened them, all I saw was acceptance, understanding.

Sid was standing next to me, not touching me but there waiting if I needed him. I sucked in a shuddery breath. "Fuck, you know my story. You don't need to hear it again." I twisted and lifted the pile of envelopes that held their wishes.

A tense silence fell as I held out the envelopes. "These are my way of sayin' thanks for bein' my family."

"If you're sharin' your millions," Razor shouted from the back of the room, "can you get Benny a new sense of humor."

Benny stuck his middle finger up at Razor as the room erupted into laughter.

"I ain't got that much cash," I quipped back. That got more laughter and released a little of the tension in the room. I walked around to a hushed silence as I gave out the named envelopes before returning to Linc and Mason.

I'd never asked either man what they'd wanted, so I'd made a calculated guess with Nutty's help. I handed the last envelope to Mason. His eyes widened before he flipped it over and peeled it open. His grin was massive as he glanced at Linc. "It's a trip to Las Vegas for *two*." Linc opened his mouth, and Mason didn't give him a chance to ask about River. "Nutty will look after River for four days."

Linc turned in Nutty's direction, and she gave him a big thumbs up before ripping open her own envelope. There was a glint in Linc's eyes I often saw in Sid's when he looked at me. Linc stared at Mason, the sexual tension between them something I didn't need to witness. Sid must have been of the same mind as he pulled me off to one side when the whole room seemed to erupt with noise all at once.

Sid grinned at me. "Look at them all. They're actin' like a bunch of five-year-olds on Christmas morning." He shook his head.

I didn't have an answer to that because my father wouldn't have tolerated this lack of control, even from a five-year-old. I sighed and shoved the old hurts back where they belonged in the past.

The loud shout that came from Cammy pulled me out of my head. "You fucker! You got Angela Davison to do a commissioned piece of artwork for me." The man bounced on his seat like an excited puppy which was hard for a guy who was six foot four and built.

There were similar cries from others. The enthusiasm was palpable as I watched grown men and women gush over the gifts I'd worked to get for each of them.

Sid nudged my shoulder. "Was it worth the effort?" He'd seen how stressed I'd gotten at times when things hadn't always gone to plan.

I turned my back on the chaos to cup Sid's face, chuckling at his startled expression as I leaned in and kissed him. "Yes, it was worth the effort."

His eyes lit up as he got what I was saying, the lines deepening as his face became serious. "It is."

Thank you for reading Sid and Toad's story. This might be the end or if you like the beginning for them, but I promise there will be more set in the world. If you want to try something different from me, then read on for something from the first book in Billionaire's Playground Series, Property of a Billionaire.

Griffin

"How did I get talked into doing this?" I grumbled as I strode down the busy corridor full of students. With my packed schedule already bursting at the seams, this was the last place I wanted to be, making the constant chatter all the more annoying.

"The same way you get roped into anything, you don't read your emails properly before you send a response," May replied.

Her curt tone was doing little to make me feel better about giving a talk, about myself and my business acumen, at Brighton University.

May stopped mid-step as I snarled at a girl who'd stepped into my path without looking where she was going. She'd been too busy staring at her phone screen to notice my approach, or that I'd had to jump out of the way to avoid bumping into her. While I was avoiding her, I hadn't seen the guy coming the other way and knocked right into him.

He "hrumphed" loudly as we collided, my hands reaching out to steady him while my gaze was still fixed on the girl already walking away.

"Why don't they bloody ban phones in school?" I seethed to no one in particular, too ticked off to notice that I was still holding onto the guy I'd walked into.

"What are you, the phone police? And I think you can let go now, mate," came a voice that instantly caught my attention. The soft Scottish brogue was all too familiar to me as I turned my attention to the man staring at me through dark-framed glasses. His grey-green eyes were quite the sucker punch, shocking me into silence, my tongue feeling too thick for my mouth as he tugged his arms from my slack fingers. His shaggy chestnut-brown hair framed a face with a stunning bone structure. Although, he had a nerdy geek look about him, there was something captivating about him. The tip of his tongue appeared and licked his full, pink lower lip, drawing my gaze.

Why are you staring at his lips?

"You know it's rude to stare, right?" The guy interrupted my thoughts, his voice taking on a sharp edge. Self-preservation kicked in and I lowered my eyelashes, needing to hide my confusion at the strange reaction I'd had to him, even in the standard university attire of baggy jeans, trainers and a hoodie.

What would his body look like underneath those baggy clothes?

What the fuck! Why would you even be interested in knowing that?

Taking an involuntary step back, I cursed at May's, more than noticeable, chuckle at my obvious discomfort. The woman was a menace and missed nothing.

The guy, on the other hand, just eyed me like I was a simpleton as my fingernails dug into my palms. "I apologise," I rasped, working at retaining an aura of calm I definitely didn't feel. I was pissed at how croaky I sounded, but resigned to it being the best that I could offer right then.

"Yeah, whatever," the guy muttered as he moved to go past me.

Unsure where the sudden urge to ask his name came from, I clamped my lips together and focused on looking forward.

"Are you quite finished trying to knock people over?" May's brows rose and disappeared under her dark, blunt fringe.

"Oh, shut up," I growled as I stomped down the corridor without waiting to see if she'd followed.

The head of the university had given me directions to his office, so I knew where to go as I dodged several more students not paying attention. But a pair of grey-green eyes behind nerdy glasses wouldn't leave me in peace.

There was something about the guy's geeky appearance that had felt slightly off, like it was a shield of some sort hiding what lay beneath.

What is it with you? Why are you even thinking about the guy? What difference does it make if he's hiding a part of himself? You do that all the time.

My teeth ground together as an image of my father escaped the barrier I'd erected to keep my past where it should remain, locked in a vault never to be looked at again. *Yeah, like it's that easy.*

This time, my jaw ached with the force of locking my teeth together.

A gentle touch to my arm distracted me and I looked towards May. The pinched expression and anxiety in her eyes forced me to take a deep breath, and then another, as I worked to loosen the rising tension.

"I'm fine," I ground out sharply before sighing. "Sorry... it's just..." I trailed off, unsure why my past was suddenly at the forefront of my mind.

"It's okay, Grif. Just give yourself a minute and take a breath." Her softly spoken words and the gentle hand rubbing at my tense forearm helped me to do as she'd requested.

As the tension eased, I gave her a smile and hoped it would be enough to stop any questions. There were only two people who knew about my past and May was one of them. The other was, what many people would refer to as my fairy godfather, Alexander McDonald, the multi-billionaire who'd taken it upon himself to rescue me from hell.

The door, several feet away from me, opened and a guy with silver hair and a navy pinstriped suit appeared. Recognising the man, I pushed away the disquiet that had clung to me ever since I'd stared into that pair of grey-green eyes. "Hello William. I'm sorry I'm running a little behind." I offered my hand as he stepped towards me.

"It's fine, you're here now. I was just on my way to the lecture theatre so it's perfect timing, Griffin." After pumping my hand enthusiastically several times, he ushered me back up the corridor

I'd just come down. It remained busy as we moved through the crowd of students still milling around.

"What are they waiting for?"

"The classes are staggered so that students have enough time to get across campus. If they don't have classes on opposite sides of the building then students tend to congregate in the halls."

It was only as William responded that I realised I'd spoken the question aloud.

His narrow shoulders shrugged as he continued to guide me through the throng of conversing students. My gaze skimmed over the young men and women standing around, searching their faces. I swallowed a sigh of disgust when I realised who I was looking for. *What are you playing at?*

Fuck knows.

The knots that had started to develop in my gut, tightened. Dismissing the urge to rub my abdomen, I turned my attention to what William was saying.

"The class you are about to talk to are all third-year students, who are doing a masters in economics and business management."

I nodded, not sure what he wanted me to say. I'd never gone to university. I'd had the life of hard knocks to provide all my lessons. That was until Alexander had shown up and decided I needed to change my ways. It had been years before I'd trusted that he only ever had my best interests at heart. The abuse and lack of anything other than hate had been so ingrained that I'd not believed that there could be someone who only wanted the best for me.

Why are you thinking about this now?

It had been years since I'd thought about my past, preferring to keep that shit where it belonged. At a loss for the reason why, a pair of grey-green eyes popped into my head, my stride faltering. I caught May's eye as she glanced my way, her pencil brows meeting in the middle. I gave her a tight smile and willed away the vivid eyes that somehow had imprinted in my mind.

I breathed a sigh of relief as William stopped at the end of yet another long hallway, apparently oblivious to my inner turmoil. We were stood in front of a broad set of doors which led into a huge lecture theatre. As we stepped into the room, the noise barely dipped.

I calculated that there had to be around a hundred students seated in the tiered seating, which was arranged in three blocks, each separated by an aisle made up of those annoying stairs that were too big to achieve in one step, but not big enough to warrant two. Down at the front of the room, there was a dais with a speaker's lectern, as well as a table and four chairs. The table held two microphones and a jug of water with several glasses.

As William stepped up onto the dais, the sound of chatting voices decreased and I was impressed that he hadn't needed to say anything in order to get the students to quieten down. My mood improved at the show of respect. That was until I reached William and turned around to face the room. As my gaze swept the sea of faces staring at me, I instantly latched onto a pair of dark-rimmed glasses which didn't conceal the widening, grey-green eyes beneath them.

The guy I'd knocked into was sitting right there in the front row. There was no way I was going to be able to avoid him.

Shitting hell, what was he doing here?

What the fuck do you think he's doing here? Waiting to listen to you talk bullshit!

Other books by the author

Standalone
When Fake Changed Everything
Christmas beyond Christmas
The Elves and the Bondage Daddy (Grim and Sinister
Delights Book 5)

Series
The Potters Creek Series
A Christmas Wish (book one)

The App Series
The App: Daddy kink (book one)
The App: Littles (book two)
The App: Puppy play (book three)

The Flamingo Bar Series
Always More (book one)
The Little Side of Me (book two)
3 Is the Magic Number (book three)

La Trattoria Di Amore Series
Puzzle Pieces (book one)
Dominated but not Subdued (book two)
Made to Submit (book three)

The Playroom Series
Mine, Body and Soul: Part One
Mine, Body and Soul: Part Two
Mine, Body and Soul: Part Three
Ferron's Journey: Damaged Part One (book four)
Ferron's Journey: Hidden Part Two (book five)

Ferron's Journey: Revelation Part Three (book six)
Mine, Body and Soul Trilogy
Ferron's Journey Trilogy

Dark River Stone Collective Series
The Light Beneath the Dark (Book One)

The Billionaire Playground Series
Property of a Billionaire (Book one)
Reluctant Billionaire (Book two)
Billionaire's Muse (Book three) coming July 2021

The Manx Cat Guardians Series
Where it all Began: Origins (Book 1)
Seeing Beyond the Scars (Book 2)
Destiny Collides Past and Present (Book 3)
Searching for a Soul to Love (Book 4)
The 12 Disasters of Christmas (Book 5)
Laws of Attraction (Book 6)
The Teacher's Boy (Book 7)
Boxset

Audio Books
Mine, Body and Soul, Part One: The Playroom Series
Mine, Body and Soul, Part Two: The Playroom Series
Mine, Body and Soul, Part Three: The Playroom
Daddy Kink: The App (book one)
Always More: The Flamingo Bar (book one)
When Fake Changed Everything
Ferron's Journey: Damaged Part One
Ferron's Journey: Hidden Part Two
Ferron's Journey: Revelation Part Three

About the author

Eccentric cake lover who has a passion for words of all kinds. I'm Jayne or JP, I live in the Isle of Man. A tiny place in the Irish sea where all the magic happens. I'm a confessed bookaholic and if I'm not writing I love to snuggle with a book or two...you catch my drift.

If you're interested in keeping up to date, then I've a few places you can do that and there listed below. If you would like to give me any feedback or just have any questions, go ahead and friend me on Facebook, and I would be happy to answer anything. Well, almost anything. I hope you enjoyed this book and if you would also like to leave a review, then I would love to read your thoughts.

THANK YOU FOR BEING A PART OF MY DREAM.